PARADOX

PARADOX

by

D.L. Line

PARADOX

ISBN 13: 978-1-62639-490-2

This Trade Paperback Original Is Published By
Bold Strokes Books, Inc.
P.O. Box 249
Valley Falls, NY 12185

First Edition: January 2015

CREDITS
EDITOR: CINDY CRESAP
PRODUCTION DESIGN: SANDY LOWE
COVER DESIGN: LEE LIGON

Dedication

For everyone who continues to help and support me, especially Christina.

CHAPTER ONE

Terri watched through the second-story window, fighting hard against her own panic and the almost blinding pain to keep her weapon trained on the psychotic killer who was holding Jen against the doorframe of her own bedroom with a loaded gun up her nose. She adjusted her grip on her sweat-slick weapon, squeezed her left eye closed to line up the sights on the slide of the gun, and pulled the trigger.

Nothing.

Terri pulled it again. A shot rang out, but she quickly realized, from the lack of recoil, that the blast hadn't come from her own SIG Sauer P-228 handgun. She stared at her weapon, until now always so reliable, and her hand began to shake. She looked up to the second floor window and the source of the shot. No matter how much she wanted to look away, she was drawn to the gory, bright red spray of blood splashed across the unbroken white of the drywall. Her ears registered the sound of a small body as it hit the landing of the stairway, impacting with a dull thud.

Oh, God, no.

Terri struggled to breathe against the racing of her own heart as it threatened to explode from her chest, and her brain struggled to make sense of the carnage that she'd just witnessed. She became dimly aware, through the intense mix of sensation and emotion, of the ring tone of a cell phone.

Her phone.

She fought toward consciousness while the phone rang a second time. Heart still pounding, Terri felt around blindly for the offending piece of technology as she tried to awaken and calm herself. She flipped the phone open with her thumb.

"Hello?"

"Terri, where are you? I thought you were meeting us at the bar. We were getting worried about you."

She pulled herself fully awake, pulse still racing, and looked around the darkened media room of her own Dupont Circle townhouse. No white farmhouse, no dew-dampened lawn, just her own leather couch. Home. "Sorry, Bobby. I fell asleep on the sofa. Give me a few minutes. I'll be right there."

"Well, Agent McKinnon, you'd better put a wiggle on it and get over here to claim your girlfriend. She's getting a lot of attention from these college kids."

Terri finally relaxed enough to laugh. "Yes, sir, Agent Kraft. Keep an eye on her for me. I'll be right there."

Attempting to will away the last images of the extremely vivid nightmare that had broken the peace of her nap, Terri closed the phone after Bobby said his good-byes. Still shaking, she dragged herself up off the sofa and headed for the bathroom to freshen up and get out the door.

Six months.

It had been six months since that fateful night, somewhere

in the mountainous, rural farmlands of western Virginia. So much had changed since then.

She pulled her hair back in a loose ponytail and splashed some cold water on her face. Jen was alive and happy, the bad guy was dead, and Terri had spent many uncomfortable hours during the last six months trying to figure out what to do about her continuing nightmares. Yes, the bad guy was dead, but only because Terri had killed him. She knew she should draw comfort from the fact that her actions had been necessary. If she hadn't pulled the trigger, Jen would be dead. However, the nightmares continued, and though they came with less frequency, they were just as horrific. The gory details remained undiluted by the passage of time.

The late September night was warm, and the outside air helped her to clear the last vestiges of the nightmare as she walked the four blocks down Connecticut Avenue. She heard the music before she even rounded the corner. The evening was filled with the sounds of the busy Dupont Circle neighborhood of Washington, DC, augmented by the driving dance beat of the nearby bar. Terri braced herself for the volume of the club as she pulled the door open and walked inside.

She searched the large, smoke-filled room until her eyes met with the dark brown ones of her partner Bobby, who waved her over as he took a swig of beer and continued cruising the club's patrons. As she picked her way through the frenzied dancers, Terri laughed a little to herself. She knew exactly what he was looking for. She was here for a different reason. Well, not exactly different. He was in the club to hook up with a yet unnamed boy in tight jeans. She was here to hook up with the bartender. The really cute little bartender with auburn hair, decked in Levi's

501 jeans and a tight black T-shirt that advertised the American University Gay/Straight Student Alliance, who also happened to be Jen, her girlfriend and assistant professor of the American University Department of Information Technology.

Terri squeezed her way past the last couple of androgynous college students, lost in the music, and landed in front of Bobby. He pulled her close in order to talk over the noise of the club, and pointed to Jen. "I didn't know she could do that. She's really good at it."

"Yeah, she is. She told me that she worked at a bar for extra cash while she was in grad school at MIT, so she was pretty excited about working for the Alliance fundraiser."

"How's that going to work?"

Terri watched Jen as she shouted over the noise to answer Bobby's question. "The Alliance provides the bartenders. They get to keep the cover charge and any tips that they get before ten p.m. After that, the regular staff takes over..."

"And you get to go home with the cute bartender."

"Yeah, I get to go home with the cute bartender. It helps that she's the faculty advisor for the Alliance."

Bobby laughed. "And those 501s don't hurt either."

"No, Bobby, they don't hurt in the least."

Terri checked her watch, noting that it was almost time for the regular staff to take over the bartending duties. The crowd was thick with boisterous college students and the denizens of the Circle, but Terri saw no one but Jen, as she set up glasses, filled them with ice, and began upending bottles with a practiced ease that Terri found to be frankly sexy. And she again noted that Bobby was absolutely right about the button fly jeans. She checked her watch again and realized that she'd been so mesmerized by Jen's bar skills and hot back pockets that she hadn't even bothered to approach and order a drink. Well, that situation needed to be rectified. She patted Bobby on the arm, wished him "happy hunting," and edged her way through the crowd toward the other end of the bar.

Climbing onto a recently vacated barstool, Terri caught Jen's attention and was treated with a smile that lit a special place in her soul every time she saw it. Jen turned and pulled a bottle of Bombay Sapphire Gin from the back bar and pointed to it, silently asking Terri if she'd like her usual drink. Terri acknowledged the offer and watched Jen reach for a tall highball glass, fill it with ice, pour a generous amount of the top-shelf liquor over it, and use the soda gun to fill the glass with tonic water. Jen slid the glass across the bar and hollered over the noise, "Hey, baby."

"Hey, you. How's it going?" Terri pulled a twenty-dollar bill out of her pocket and slid it across the bar. Jen attempted to wave it off, but Terri insisted. "Ring it up and put the change in the bucket for the Alliance. Are you almost finished?"

Jen checked the Budweiser clock over the bar. "Ten minutes, then we do the money thing with the manager, and I'm out of here. Just sit tight and I'll check back in when I'm done."

Terri raised her glass and swiveled the barstool. She spotted Bobby in the corner, stalking his prey, and decided to leave him to his activities for the evening. Time passed quickly while Terri watched people dance and mingle. Before she knew it, she felt a warm hand on her shoulder and heard Jen's voice in her ear. "I'm all done. Do you want to stay?"

Terri was feeling overwhelmed by the crowd and the noise, so she shook her head, drained the last bit of her drink, and allowed herself to be led by the hand through the busy club and out the door. As they headed out into the clear night air, Terri relaxed a little and decided to properly greet Jen by dragging her around the corner to the end of the alley, wrapping her arms around her waist, and pulling her close for a warm, wet kiss. Jen melted into the kiss, leaning forward until Terri's back was pressed against the brick wall. A mutual need for air forced them to stop.

Jen repeated her greeting from earlier, "Hey, baby."

"Hey, you. Did you have a good night?"

Jen stayed close, hanging onto Terri's belt loops. "It's better now. You were late. I was worried about you."

"Sorry, I kind of fell asleep on the sofa. It's been a long week."

"Yeah, it has been, but it's Friday and we have the whole weekend to relax. Whatever shall we do with ourselves?"

Terri slid her hands into the back pockets of the blue jeans that had held her interest for so much of the evening, pulled Jen closer, and answered, "Actually, I have some ideas about what I'd like to do to you."

"My, my, Agent McKinnon, care to share?"

Terri nuzzled in under Jen's chin, nipping lightly around her neck, as Jen closed her eyes and allowed her head to roll back. "Well, I thought maybe I could—"

"Dr. Rosenberg?"

Terri stopped mid-nuzzle, surprised by the sound of an unfamiliar voice. She felt Jen's attempt to back away. Evidently, she was surprised as well by the fact that they weren't as alone as they had assumed. She removed her hands from Jen's pockets and also attempted to back away but was stopped by the brick wall behind her.

The unfamiliar voice said, "Wow, Dr. Rosenberg. Way to go."

A red glow crawled up Jen's face, and Terri processed that the comment had not come from a stranger, but from someone that Jen knew. Jen's response confirmed it. "Umm, hi, Denny. Here for the fundraiser?"

Terri was now in full agent mode, watching as Denny answered.

"Um, yeah, but I'm kind of late." Terri was well aware of the fact that she was being studied as well, but relaxed a little as Jen remembered her manners and began the introductions.

"Terri, this is Denise Robertson, but everyone calls her Denny. You know, my new graduate assistant." Remembering her own manners, Terri extended her hand to the woman. "Denny, this is my girlfriend, Terri McKinnon. Sorry, I forgot that you two haven't met yet." Terri felt the strong grip as her handshake was returned, and they exchanged a friendly nod and smile.

Denny backed away, motioning toward the door of the club with both thumbs. "Well, I should probably go inside. Besides, I think I was interrupting. You two have a good evening." Before she left, she grinned at Terri again. "It was nice to meet you." She shot a cheeky wink toward Jen. "I'll see you Monday, Dr. Rosenberg."

Denny rounded the corner and disappeared from view. Turning her attention toward Jen, Terri noted the reappearance of a slight blush on the freckled cheeks. "And where did she play softball?"

It was apparent that Terri's assumption was correct as the

tinge of red turned to flame. "She was a shortstop at James Madison and was in a couple of my classes there last year. She's really bright, so when I spotted her records on the top of the pile, I thought she'd be a great assistant."

Terri could only laugh as she recalled Jen's history with softball players.

"Agent McKinnon, I am fully aware of exactly where and how my bread gets buttered, so you have nothing to worry about. Besides, Denny was right. She was interrupting. I believe you were about to tell me about something really interesting that you wanted to do this weekend."

Terri gave her one last nip to the neck. "I think I'd rather show you." She took Jen by the hand and led her down the alley back toward Connecticut Avenue. "C'mon. Let's go home."

CHAPTER TWO

A thunderous wall of sound echoed through the desert as the weapons facility was obliterated in a fiery ball of destruction. Smoke rolled across the unbroken stretch of sun-baked earth, engulfing everything in its path, cactus and Gila monster alike. A second blast erupted, followed quickly by a third and a fourth, as the fireball reached the all-terrain vehicles parked around the flaming hulk of exploded timber and cinderblock, igniting their gas tanks in a booming celebration of carnage.

Then silence.

A deafening quiet followed the sound, as the cacophony of smoke and noise was carried away by the prevailing winds. Nothing moved. Nothing with the exception of a lone figure, clad from top to toe in black, from the wide straps of a tank top to the roomy functionality of a pair of well-fitting cargo pants to the tightly wrapped laces of a pair of hard-worn combat boots. As the figure emerged from the smoke, details became more distinct. Handguns, a matched set of Desert Eagle Mark XIX automatics, unused but ready if necessary, strapped securely to *the thighs of the figure. A crossbelt of black military webbing, loaded with extra 9-round clips and a rather large, deadly-looking Dark Ops fighting knife, nestled neatly between the shapely breasts of the commando. Chocolate brown hair, pulled back into a loose ponytail framed the figure's face, eyes hidden by a pair of Ray-Ban Flight Extreme sunglasses.*

A rhythmic, insistent tapping sound drew the attention of the deadly commando. She threw the electronic detonator gripped tightly in her right hand to the side, its necessity gone with the fireball that had consumed the squat concrete building. Turning her attention to the source of the sound, the commando pulled a Mossberg 590 Compact Cruiser shotgun around from its back strap, snapped it quickly up and then back down, and chambered the round with a smooth, one-handed move. Firing once at the noise, she pulled the powerful weapon up again; muscles rippling as another one-handed pump chambered the next round. She fired again as the rapping sound continued, now accompanied by a voice. A very insistent voice. She pumped the shotgun one last time, but did not fire, as the indistinct voice formed itself into actual words.

"Dr. Rosenberg?"

The beautiful, yet lethal commando lowered the hot, smoking barrel of her shotgun and reached up to remove her sunglasses. Her deep blue eyes bore straight ahead. Her voice was husky and crackled with humor.

"Hey, Rosenberg, snap out of it. You're at work."

Startled, Jen shook her head, attempting to clear the vivid images of the fantasy as she became fully aware that the disembodied voice in the desert was actually attached to a person who was now knocking at her door, requesting her attention for a second time.

"Dr. Rosenberg, are you okay?"

Jen blinked stupidly as her eyes met those of her graduate assistant Denny, standing in the open door of Jen's office. More than slightly embarrassed at being caught in the middle of a daydream instead of working, she shoved the sensations of the fantasy aside, waved Denny into her office, and attempted to apologize.

"Sorry, Denny. I was just, umm, working out a program for debugging class. I get kind of lost in that. Come in and have a seat."

Denny sat and dropped her backpack to the floor. "Wow, that must be some program to make you blush like that. I can't wait to see it."

Denny quickly clapped a hand over her mouth, seemingly surprised at her own words. Jen decided that diversion was the best plan, so she cleared her throat and changed the subject.

"So, Denny, how are things going? Do you have those lesson plans for basic programming ready?" Jen sat back and crossed her legs, attempting to ignore the last bit of the fantasy that had gathered in the crotch of her stylish, charcoal-gray pinstriped trousers.

"Umm, yeah." Denny retrieved the lesson plans from her backpack and handed them across the desk.

Jen scanned the papers quickly before setting them aside on the cluttered surface of her desk. "Thanks, I'll look those over when we're done here. How is everything else going? Are you finding your way around the city, meeting new folks, all that kind of thing?"

Denny nodded. "Yeah. My apartment is nice, and the neighbors are too. Classes are going well, and the freshmen seem to think I know what I'm talking about, so it's all good. It's really different from Harrisonburg, but I can handle it."

"It's different all right," Jen agreed. Her thoughts drifted to the process of her own relocation from the same area of western Virginia, three months earlier. "I was fortunate enough to have a tour guide, so that helped a lot."

"Yeah, that would help, but I'm managing pretty well on my own. You know, single girl, big city. It's been great."

Jen noticed the time. She had a department meeting to get to. "So is there anything else I can do for you? I kind of need to head out."

"Well, there is one more thing. I got a call the other day from someone. They offered me, well, I guess they offered me a job. The details are sort of strange, so I need some advice. It seems almost too good to be true, but the pay is good, and I really need the money."

Jen narrowed her eyes, remembering a similar shady job offer once in her past, and offered a warning. "Denny, be careful. I get that you need the money. I certainly did when I was in school, and the one offer I took wound up coming back to bite me in the ass in a really big way. I know the money is tempting, and I certainly don't have the authority to tell you what to do, but just...well, just be careful. You know what they say about things that seem too good to be true."

"Yeah, I get it. They usually are." Denny's face telegraphed her disappointment, but Jen sensed a trace of residual thought, as if she were still contemplating the idea.

"I'm serious here, Denny. I know you're twenty-three

years old and think that nothing's going to happen. Hell, I was nineteen years old and I was positive that nothing would happen. So trust me when I tell you, if a crazy person shows up at your house ten years from now and threatens to blow your brains out, you'll really wish you'd listened to me."

"What?"

"When I was an undergrad at Michigan, I learned to seriously hack from this strange guy who owned a computer shop. He showed me some pretty tricky stuff for the time, and I eventually did a little of that hacking-for-cash thing. Well, this led to that, and the guy wound up in prison, thanks to me. He got out last year and decided that he was pissed and wanted me dead. He showed up at my house and would have killed me, but Terri shot and killed him."

"Holy cow, you're serious."

"Yes, Denny, I'm very serious. But hey, look on the bright side. I got a really hot FBI agent out of the deal." Grinning weakly, Jen sat back. "Not that it's a great way to meet girls, but..."

"You mean your girlfriend is an FBI agent? Holy crap... I mean, wow, umm..." Denny sat and stared, apparently trying to come up with something else to say. "I mean, she is hot, and..."

"Yes, that she is. But that's another discussion for another time. I really do need to leave for a meeting. I'll check your plans when I get back, and e-mail you if you need to change anything. I'm sure they're fine." Jen got up from her chair, indicating that it was time for Denny to do the same.

"Okay, Dr. Rosenberg. Wow, that's a lot to think about."

Jen attempted to ease the tension in the office, "Trust me, Denny. If you need the cash, try bartending. The tips are good, and there is a greatly reduced risk of eventual bloody death. Besides, it's easier to meet girls that way; trust me."

Jen grabbed her briefcase and ushered Denny from the office. Closing the door behind her, Jen watched Denny, still shaking her head, as she headed off down the hallway. Jen grimaced to herself, remembering how very much like Denny she had once been—naïve, trusting, and called after her, "See you tomorrow."

Denny didn't even turn around. She just waved and turned to head down the steps. Jen followed soon after, inwardly hoping that her story had made the proper impact and that Denny would make the right decision. She was also well aware that Denny was one of that class of young people who tended to believe that they were bulletproof. Knowing that she'd done all that was possible for the time being, Jen hiked her briefcase higher on her shoulder and headed out the door for her meeting.

As she crossed the campus on the bright, early fall day, Jen felt buzzing in the pocket of her trousers, followed by the sound of the *Mission: Impossible* theme song. She smiled, knowing from the ring tone that Terri was the caller, and answered. "Hey, you. What's up?"

"Hey, you too. Not a lot. I just wanted to check in and see how your day was going."

"Great. I'm actually on my way to a meeting over at the faculty lunchroom. I was thinking about you earlier."

"What was it this time? Was I blowing stuff up in the desert again?"

"Well, umm, yeah... kind of."

"Oh, God, Jen. You have such an imagination."

"That's not a complaint I hear, is it, Agent McKinnon?"

Terri sighed heavily, her amusement replaced by something else. "No, it's not. You know, I just worry that—"

"I know very well what you worry about," Jen interrupted, "and we've had this conversation before. I am perfectly content with you, the real you. I just have a vivid imagination and there are no expectations on my part that you leave the FBI and become some kind of Siberian mercenary. I love you just the way you are, so you can really stop worrying any time now. Okay?"

"Okay, I believe you. It's silly anyway. Never mind. Actually, I did call for a reason. Do you mind if Bobby comes over for dinner tonight? He's been a little moody lately, so I asked him over to talk."

"Is he all right?"

"Well, I think so, but this isn't like him, so I thought I'd try to find out what's going on. You know I can always bribe him to talk when there's food involved."

"Yes, I am well aware of the power of your culinary skills. Of course, baby, that's fine. Do you need me to stop at the store on the way home?"

"I don't think...oh, wait. If you could stop and get a loaf of bread and a bottle of wine for us, that would be great. There's beer in the fridge for Bobby, and I already have the other stuff for dinner."

"Check. Loaf of bread and a bottle of wine. You want red or white?"

"Sweetie, whatever you like. Either is fine."

Jen checked her watch. "Okay, I'll see what strikes me when I get to the store. I have to go... meeting, you know."

"Oh, right. Go to your meeting and I'll see you around five.

I love you."

Jen felt the flutter in her chest that she always did when she heard that last little phrase. "I love you too. See you later."

Jen snapped her phone closed after Terri said good-bye, and headed into her meeting, hoping that it would be short and interesting enough to keep the Siberian mercenary images at bay. It never was, but she could still hope.

CHAPTER THREE

Terri sat quietly at her new desk on the fourth floor of the J. Edgar Hoover FBI Building. Twiddling a pen in her left hand, she looked over the paperwork for her last, recently-closed case. Making sure that all the I's were dotted and the T's were crossed, she signed the report, tucked it into its folder, and leaned back to stretch. That was done. Now what?

Terri looked across her desk, catching Bobby's attention. He pointed at the folder containing the completed report. "What's up? You done with that?"

"Yep. One more little old lady that won't ever cheat at bingo again." Terri used the now all-too-familiar sarcastic catch phrase, indicating her dismay at the constant stream of boring, dead assignments that she and Bobby had been forced to endure in the past several months. "Bobby, this sucks. Are we ever going to get a real case again?"

"How should I know, kiddo? I just do what they tell me to do and try to make the best of it. Hang in there."

"Well, I'm getting sick of hanging in there all the time. These dead-end, nothing cases are going to be the death of both of us. Especially you."

Bobby waved aside her concern. "It's cool. I've had enough excitement. I'm actually kind of enjoying the peace and quiet." He looked aside as if something on the wall was particularly interesting. Terri spotted the avoidance immediately.

"Hey, mister, I saw that. What the hell is going on with you? I've done everything, and that includes feeding you a couple of nights ago, and I get nothing. You're pissed about this, and you're not telling me something. What's that all about?"

Bobby opened his mouth to answer, but never got a chance to get the words out, as Supervisor George McNally stepped off the elevator, gruff demeanor and steel-gray brush cut intact, and summoned his agents.

"McKinnon. Kraft. My office. Now."

Terri rolled her eyes at McNally's usual lack of manners, noting that Bobby did the same. She smirked at Bobby's familiar reaction, taking some comfort in the fact that he shared her opinion regarding their boss's predictable behavior. She picked up the folder that she'd been working on and allowed herself to be ushered into McNally's office by Bobby. He closed the door behind them.

Without even looking up, McNally tossed a new folder on his desk."Have a seat."

Terri sat, crossed her legs, and laid the folder that she had been carrying across her lap. Bobby mirrored her actions, and sat back, waiting for McNally to continue.

"Are those reports complete?" McNally held out his hand to collect the reports. "Good... thank you. Now, I have something new for you."

Terri sat forward, eager to get back to work on a case that

might be just the least bit interesting. She noted that McNally exchanged a look with Bobby, but opted to allow it to go.

McNally slid the new folder across his desk, sat back, and pointed to it. "That is the preliminary report from the Centreville Police Department regarding a small warehouse company. Apparently, one of the secretaries in the company did a little whistle-blowing on her employers, alleging the misuse of federal postal channels."

Terri's mouth fell open in shock. "Mail fraud? Another case of mail fraud? You've got to be kidding."

She cringed at the inappropriateness of her reaction, and braced for McNally's response.

"Agent McKinnon, as you were," McNally ordered through gritted teeth. "This is the case you need to work on, and there will be no further discussion."

She looked to Bobby for support, but he avoided her glance, apparently finding the view out the window over McNally's left shoulder more interesting. What was going on here? She attempted to collect herself enough to continue without further pissing off the boss. "But, sir—"

"No buts, Agent McKinnon. This is your assignment." Terri stared at him, dumbstruck as McNally stared right back. This was usually the point in the conversation that McNally said thank you and expected his agents to leave, but he surprised Terri by doing something different. "Agent Kraft, please get started on this." He slid the folder to Bobby, who picked it up and set it across his lap. "And would you please give Agent McKinnon and me a moment alone? Thank you."

Bobby tucked the folder under his arm and got up to leave the office, avoiding the glare Terri was pointedly shooting at him. The door closed behind him, and Terri turned her attention to McNally, who was leaning back as far as his office chair would allow, cradling the back of his head with his hands, studying Terri intently.

"Agent McKinnon... Terri..." She started inwardly at McNally's use of her first name. "We, that is to say, you have a problem. I just got the latest report regarding your fitness for duty from the head shrinkers upstairs, and you still haven't been cleared to return to regular duty. That's why I've had to give you and Agent Kraft all the shit cases."

McNally's words were like a bucket of ice water dumped on her anger. She looked up, struggling to collect herself, and tried to piece together a response. "But, sir, I don't understand. I've gone to the appointments, talked about everything. I'm good to go here."

"Well, the folks upstairs don't share your opinion, and until something up there changes, there's nothing I can do. I can only suggest that you make another appointment and just keep talking to them." He sat forward, offering out his hands in a supplicating gesture. "I'm sorry, Terri, but my hands are tied. This is up to you to fix. The report says that you are still too great a risk to be in a hazardous situation. Until that report comes back squeaky clean, I can't put you out there with a loaded weapon in your hands. I can't be sure that you'll use it if the situation requires it."

Terri stared at him with absolutely no idea what to say next. She sat, noting inwardly that her anger was almost gone, replaced by a deep sadness that she was clueless how to deal with.

"Terri, you know that things haven't been right since you

shot that perp on the Rosenberg case. I was uncomfortable about it at the time, and things aren't any better now. I know that the fact that he shot you first doesn't make it any easier, but I let you go off cowboy-style on something that I was unsure of, and you almost got yourself and Agent Kraft killed. I will assume partial responsibility for the situation, but I can't fix it. That's up to you."

Terri allowed McNally's words to sink in. She couldn't argue with him because she knew deep down that he was right. There was no way she would allow anyone in the office, especially McNally, to see her cry, but it took all the resolve she had to keep it from happening.. "Yes, sir. I understand. I'll take care of that right away. Thank you."

McNally allowed a small smile, breaking his granite façade. "Yes, Agent McKinnon, I know you will. Now, go catch me an evil stamp collector. Thank you." He directed his attention to the screen of his computer, indicating to Terri that she could leave. She opened the door to his office and stepped back into the shared space of the Investigations Department, quietly pulling the door closed behind her.

Terri crossed the space to return to her desk; the desk that she now feared that she would be chained to forever, and waited for Bobby to look at her. He just kept studying the new case file, apparently unwilling to meet her insistent gaze. "Bobby, you knew about this, didn't you?"

He closed the file on his desk, raising his head just enough to look her in the eye. "Yeah, Terri, I did."

As the deep sadness settled in for a long stay, Terri felt the anger begin to bubble up again. "And you couldn't be bothered to tell me, right?"

"Sweetie, no, it wasn't like that at all. McNally wanted to see me on Monday, so that's why I came in early. He gave me the lowdown and offered me a choice. He also told me not to say anything to you until he had a chance to talk to you about it. Don't you think I would have told you otherwise?"

Bobby's words went a long way toward calming her rage. "You know, I'm not sure what I think about anything right now. You'll understand that I'm feeling a little cornered here."

"Yeah, I get that. And I don't blame you, but there was nothing I could do. Sweetie, I went to bat for you. I really did, but it's not up to me or McNally. You need to get this straightened out with the witch doctors upstairs, or we're going to be on the old-ladies-cheating-at-bingo circuit until we're the old ladies cheating at bingo. I know you don't want that and neither do I."

"What do you mean? They're just going to keep you chained here with me. That's not terribly comforting."

"Well, maybe you should take some comfort from that. They must think you'll come around soon, or McNally wouldn't have offered me a choice. He told me that I could stay on the shit jobs with you or else he was going to break us up. I didn't want that, and I don't think you do either, so I'll wait for you as long as I have to."

Terri's anger was now fully gone, leaving nothing but sadness. "But, Bobby, what about your career? You just can't sit here forever and wait for me."

His disarming grin almost made her feel better. "Kiddo, I know you're going to kick this thing in the ass, and I think it's going to be soon. I'm here for you, just like I have been since day one. Anything you need, you know all you have to do is ask. So I think it's time for you to screw on your best, what is it that

Jen calls it? Your G-man mojo?" Terri nodded as he continued, "Call those head shrinkers and go take care of this thing, okay?"

Terri finally allowed herself a small smile. Bobby really was a great friend, and she hoped that he was right this time. Her answer was to sit down at her desk, pick up the phone, dial the switchboard, and ask to be connected to the agent support department. Finally, they answered and scheduled the appointment for her. After she hung up the phone, she wrote the appointment time on her calendar and grabbed her wallet from her briefcase.

"Bobby, I'm going downstairs to get something to eat." She pointed to the file on his desk. "Can that wait for a little while?"

"Sure. Nothing earth-shattering here. Do you want some company?"

"Thank you, Bobby, but no. I need a little time to process this. I'd be lousy company right now. Okay?"

"Okay, Kiddo. But remember, anything you need."

"Yeah, I get it." Terri got up from her desk and left the office. She walked down the hall to the elevator, her throat tightening with each step. She pushed the button, waited a few seconds for the doors to open, and stepped inside. The doors closed and Terri was finally alone, and once the tears started, she wasn't sure that she could stop them any time soon.

Chapter Four

Terri sat quietly on a black vinyl-covered sofa leafing through a magazine. Page after page of nothing interesting, but it was better than twiddling her thumbs. The receptionist, a completely unremarkable woman of late middle age, worked diligently at the computer on her desk. She would occasionally glance over and smile, but for the most part, left Terri alone to idly flip pages and not read the magazine. She stopped flipping to look at a picture.

Oh my God, these two just don't stop. Maybe I could pretend to be a Cambodian baby and then I wouldn't be sitting here now. Yeah, Terri, that's the attitude. You want your life back and now you're worrying about Brad and Angelina. Get a grip.

Terri tossed the magazine on the table with a small huff of frustration. The receptionist looked up and smiled again, and Terri did her best not to stick out her tongue.

She knows why I'm here. Hell, I might just as well have "defective agent" stamped on my forehead. Let's get on with this already.

The phone rang sharply on the receptionist's desk, startling them both. Midway through the second ring, the receptionist picked up the handset and answered with a cheery, "Yes, Doctor." The person on the other end kept it short, and the receptionist hung up the phone. "Agent McKinnon?"

Terri looked up in response.

"She's ready for you." She pointed to a door to her left. "Right through there."

Terri got up from the sofa and crossed the small space, every step filling her with just a little more apprehension. "Thank you. I remember." The receptionist returned to her work on the computer and Terri turned the knob, pushed the door open, stepped into the office, and closed the door behind her, wishing she were anywhere else but here. Meeting yet another new therapist who would no doubt tell her she still had more processing to do. Great.

Another middle-aged woman, younger and slightly more attractive than the receptionist, stood up from the high-backed office chair behind her desk, nondescript manila folder in her left hand, and greeted Terri by extending her right hand and introducing herself.

"Agent McKinnon, it's nice to meet you. Why don't you have a seat and let's get started." Terri accepted the closer of the two chairs facing the desk, taking note of the assortment of Native American artifacts on the shelves and large Navajo rug hanging on the wall. New stuff since her last visit, but the face of the therapist was new also, so she dismissed it quickly.

Terri sat and crossed her legs, attempting to make herself as comfortable as possible. Considering that Terri was somewhere she didn't want to be doing something she didn't want to do, any kind of comfortable was pretty much out the window. She settled in as much as she could and waited for the doctor, who finally broke the silence.

"Well, Agent McKinnon... Terri. May I call you Terri?"

Does it matter?

"Sure. That's fine."

The therapist pushed the closed file folder out of her way in order to weave her fingers together and lean her forearms on the neat-as-a-pin surface of her desk. "Well then, Terri, since I'm new here and this is the first chance I've had to talk with you, how about we start with the basics? It seems the Bureau is concerned about your actions on a case from several months ago. I've read the report, but I'm more interested in your views. What happened there?" *Besides me falling into a relationship with the victim?*

"Well, it was a standard stalking case that involved a recently-released convict who wanted to exact some revenge on the person who, in his opinion, landed him in prison. He committed a series of crimes ranging from simple battery to arson, killing two people along the way."

"That seems pretty straightforward. Did something unusual happen?"

Unusual. That's a great word. He tried to murder my girlfriend.

"There was an interesting aspect to the case when the fire department found a body in the basement of his fourth crime scene, an arson attempt. He had duped someone, set him up as a decoy, switched ID, and allowed him to die in the fire. It seemed wrong for his profile, so I questioned it."

The therapist cocked her head to one side and furrowed her brow. "What do you mean, you questioned it?"

You mean, besides looking for any excuse I could find to stay and protect her?

Terri inhaled deeply and resigned herself to telling the story that she had already told so many times. "There were heavy amounts of alcohol and prescription medications in the body, and it just seemed wrong to me. The perpetrator had eluded us for weeks, and I knew he was smarter than that. I questioned the identification of the body and went to my boss with it."

"And he approved your actions?"

Well, yes, if you mean he accused me of behaving inappropriately and lying to him, which I was and I did.

"Yes. There were some issues with the local sheriff since there was evidence to support the removal of their backup. That left my partner and me out there on our own. I'm sure McNally—he's my supervisor—thought I was wrong or else he wouldn't have left us out there like that."

"How do you feel about that?"

Hung out to dry for attempting to protect someone I love more than anything.

"It's policy. I understood the consequences, and I felt our continued presence was worth the risk." Terri fidgeted in her seat, intently studying the spines of the books on the shelf behind the therapist. She knew that she was being studied as well, so managed to maintain a calm façade, despite her desire to be anywhere but where she was.

"Were you right about the dupe?"

You're goddamned right I was.

"Yes, it turned out that I was correct and the perpetrator showed up on the target's property the next evening. My partner and I set up a standard perimeter watch. We patrolled for several hours until a noise in the barn alerted my partner, so he went to check it out. We lost radio contact shortly after that." Terri shifted in her seat, crossing her left ankle over her right knee to pick at the cat hair on the hem of her slacks.

"So did you call for backup when that happened?"

No, I damn near peed my pants like a little kid because I was so scared that someone was going to hurt my girlfriend that I just fucking forgot.

"No. I thought that there might be radio interference, so I opted to go look for him myself. I had no reason to believe that anything had happened to him." She sat back and returned her foot to the floor, crossing her arms over her chest.

"And did you locate him?"

Yeah, in a big useless pile on the floor.

"Yes, he had been attacked by the perpetrator, who struck him over the head with a shovel. He was unconscious, so I checked to see if I could assist him."

"So did you call for backup then?"

No. I panicked. Remember that "so scared I thought I might pee my pants" part? Stay with me here, Doc.

"No. I attempted to do so, but the perpetrator threatened me before I could. He got the drop on me while I was offering assistance to Agent Kraft."

"He threatened you how?"

God, you're just dense. He was going to steal my lunch money. What do you think?

"He threatened me with a handgun to the back of my neck." Terri tilted her head a little to the right, and pointed to the spot with her left index finger. "Right here."

"That must have been frightening."

No, it was just like rolling in big, fluffy piles of hugs and puppies. Better than sweaty, naked sex.

"Yes, it was." Terri inwardly enjoyed the therapist's shudder at the thought. They always did that.

The barrage of questions continued. "What did you do?"

Remember that "thought I would pee my pants" part? We're right back there.

"Well, my options seemed limited, until something diverted the perpetrator's attention."

"What was that?"

Twelve pounds of neutered mutt with way more balls than I had at the moment. Oh, by the way, he lives with me now.

"Jen... um, Dr. Rosenberg's dog, Snickers." Terri smiled a bit as the therapist laughed at her dog's name. "He evidently had a small problem with strangers and decided to attack Mr. Davis. I saw an opening and I reacted by attempting to strike him in the face with my weapon. Davis, not Snickers." The therapist appeared to relax a little more, as she leaned back in her chair, making non-committal noises of agreement.

"Well, I didn't think you'd find it necessary to pistol-whip a dog. But anyway, then what happened?"

Oh, you're going to love this part. I sure did.

"Then he shot me." *Damn, that hurt. That hurt a lot.* Terri hesitated in order to collect herself. The memory of the severity of her injuries, while six months old, was still pretty fresh. She took a long breath. "When I struck him, his gun went off. I was properly outfitted in a Kevlar vest, but the impact broke three of my ribs. I fell pretty hard and cut my face, too." Terri raised her hand, using her right index finger to lightly touch the scar just above her right eyebrow. "It was a big cut. Took thirteen stitches to close it. When I attempted to turn over to return his fire, the floor of the barn collapsed under me. Davis apparently thought I was either dead or too injured to bother with, so he headed up to the house."

"What did you do next? Did you call for backup?"

Jesus, here she goes again with the backup thing. Lady, I fucked up. Remember the panicked and scared part? Add bleeding and broken to that.

"No. Davis was ahead of me now and I was concerned that a large show of force would push him over the edge." *Like I was thinking of anything but getting to Jen before he did.* "I knew that he had already killed two people, so he had nothing to lose by killing one more. I determined the best course of action and dealt with the problem myself."

"How did you do that?"

I offered to let him watch us have sex if he wouldn't blow my girlfriend's brains out. What do you think I did?

"I determined that the best course of action was to attempt to remove him from the situation. I set myself up strategically and I shot him."

"And you killed him?"

Terri looked at the floor. "Yes, I killed him."

"How do you feel about that?"

Haunted, tortured, pained, disturbed. Nothing good, believe me. But then again, I ended his pathetic, waste-of-space existence before he could snuff out the light of my life.

"It was unfortunate, but there was no other option. He already had Dr. Rosenberg pinned to the wall, threatening her with his weapon. If I hadn't shot him, he would have shot her. There was no other option."

The therapist was silent for a moment. Terri watched her face, attempting to gauge her reaction to the answers she'd provided to all the stock questions. The therapist took a long moment to center herself. "I will never get used to the level of violence that you people are forced to live with every day." Since it wasn't a question, Terri sat and waited patiently to see what would happen next. The next question surprised her.

"Terri, are you married?"

What?

"No, I'm not."

"Seeing someone, dating, got a boyfriend, anything like that?"

Can I trust you?

"Yes, I am. Actually, I'm living with someone." Terri crossed her foot over her knee again and picked at some more residual cat hair around the hem of her black slacks, inwardly bracing for the next question.

"Does he have a name?"

Oh, shit. Come out, come out wherever you are. Focus, Terri. She looks okay. Go ahead. Trust her.

"Actually, she does have a name." The therapist didn't flinch, not a bit. She raised her eyebrows, silently urging Terri to continue. "Her name is Jen."

A ghost of a smile floated around the therapist's mouth for just a moment before it was replaced by a wrinkled forehead and a not so ghostly frown. "Jen... as in Dr. Jen Rosenberg?"

Big time, oh, shit. Well, it's out there now, Terri. Just do it.

"Yes, Dr. Jen Rosenberg, the target of the perpetrator that we've just spent the last few minutes talking about. She got a job offer here at American University, so she moved in with me three months ago."

"Snickers, too?"

Relax, Terri. She's okay. Really.

"Yes, Snickers too." Terri returned to the cat hair on her slacks while the therapist took a second to formulate an opinion.

"So did you start this relationship before or after the shooting?"

Good question, Doc. I can do this.

"Actually, the crimes started out as apparently random events. The only common thread was the victim's employer. Since Dr. Rosenberg was close by and worked for the same company, Agent Kraft and I interviewed her early in the investigation. Then she asked me out to dinner. Agent Kraft pushed, and I said yes. I did question the appropriateness of my own actions, but decided that since there was no hard evidence at the time to indicate that she was in any danger, I opted to pursue the relationship."

"And everything's fine with you two now? You're getting along okay? No problems?"

We're getting along finer than you could imagine. You should see her naked. Wait, no. Never mind.

The thought of a naked Jen lifted her spirits considerably. "No problems. We get along great. Everything works just fine for both of us. Her dog even likes my cat."

"Terri, I'm very happy for you. But I do understand why there was a problem, and why you're here. Why didn't you tell either of the other therapists about your relationship?"

That's another great question. I have a great answer.

"Actually, you're the only one who's ever asked. They just hammered me with questions about why I didn't call for backup. I'm still on restriction, so I guess they didn't like my answers." Terri finally stopped fidgeting and looking around the room, focusing her attention fully on the new therapist. "Do you understand? This is important to me that I be reinstated to full duty. I need to get my life back to normal."

The therapist flipped through her notes and took a deep breath. "Terri, your file says that you've been having nightmares. How is that? Are they gone?"

Oh, shit. Not this again.

"I think they're getting better. It's been a while since I've had one, so maybe they're gone. I'm not sure."

"Tell me about them. What are they like?"

Can't we talk about Jen some more? I like that better.

Terri crossed her foot over her knee again, returning it to the floor quickly as she realized that all the cat hair was gone. "Well, they're generally the same. It usually starts out with me aiming my gun at someone who is threatening Jen, and then something happens that doesn't allow me to take the shot. You know, the gun misfires, I get distracted... things like that."

"And your girlfriend winds up dead."

"Yes."

"And you say it's been a while since you've had one of these dreams. How long?"

Five days. But that doesn't sound like the right answer.

"Probably about a month."

The therapist leaned forward, resting her forearms on the surface of her desk. "So, Terri, do you know why the Bureau still considers you high risk?"

Besides the spooky dreams and the lying and the poor judgment and the almost getting everyone killed?

"Honestly, I'm not sure. I feel ready to return to full duty. My supervisor seems to believe that I'm not...well...that I'm not predictable. He's expressed his misgivings about me reacting appropriately in a hazardous situation. I think I understand why, but I really need to get back into it to prove myself."

The therapist nodded, "Okay, Terri. What I'm hearing from you is that you really want to return to full duty, but your supervisor has noticed that something in your demeanor has changed, and he's interpreting it as a weakness to act. Does that sum it up?"

"Yes."

"So if you find yourself in exactly the same situation again, you would react appropriately? You'd make the proper calls for backup and step back if the situation required it?"

Wow, that's a really loaded question.

Terri knew the right answer, so she offered it up. "Yes."

"Even if it was Jen?"

I can't answer that. Please don't make me answer that.

"I suppose."

The therapist turned her attention back to the case file on her desk. Leafing through the paperwork, she appeared to be looking for something, but Terri sensed it was more to help her think than anything. The therapist looked up and set the file down. "You see, Terri, this is the problem the way I see it. The FBI needs the answer to that last question to be 'yes,' not 'I suppose.' You know as well as I do that one of the most important weapons in the arsenal of an agent is their professional detachment, and quite frankly, you've lost a lot of yours. But you lost it because someone you care for deeply was in danger. I daresay most of us would react exactly the same way, but the

FBI needs something extra from you."

Terri could feel her hope begin to swirl away like water down the drain. This was not going to turn out in her favor, but she remained stoic as the therapist continued.

"What I would like to recommend is that you stay on restriction until we can meet again, say in about two weeks. That will give us another chance to talk, make sure the nightmares really are gone, and reevaluate. I think, most likely, that I can recommend reinstatement at that point, but I'm just not comfortable doing it right now. I hope you understand."

Terri struggled to remain professional, biting lightly on her lower lip to fight back the tears she felt stinging in the corners of her eyes. "Two weeks?"

"Can you work with that?"

Do I have a fucking choice?

"Yes, I can work with that."

CHAPTER FIVE

Amidst the swirling mass of people at the Metro Center Station, Terri attempted to sort out her own swirling emotions. Sadness, anger, and loss were all firmly entrenched in her busy brain. She needed to find something to pull her from her own depths.

"Damn it, I am not ruining Jen's evening with all this crap," she muttered to herself.

She stepped onto the escalator for the ride down to the platform, oblivious to her fellow commuters. When her train arrived, Terri wedged herself into the car between a middle-aged business-suited guy checking his e-mail on a BlackBerry and a kid in a George Washington University sweatshirt. She resisted the urge to resent them for their placid faces and normal expressions. Closing her eyes, she began rehashing her conversation with the therapist. Where had she gone wrong?

Terri was so lost in her own recriminations that she almost missed her stop, sidestepping quickly through the doors of the train as they nearly closed on her. Determined as she was to put on a good face for Jen, the prospects of that happening dimmed as she rode the long escalator up into the bright September sunshine of Dupont Circle. One simple fact remained: she was still out in the cold with the Bureau. She couldn't do her job, the one she was damn good at. Or at least she used to be. She could only trudge the three blocks home feeling lost and defeated.

As usual, Jen's green 4Runner was parked in the driveway next to the steps of their townhouse. Terri started up the steps, stopping to enjoy the sound of Snickers announcing her arrival. Since she didn't want to drag into the house looking like a depressed mess, she squared her shoulders and opened the first door. Her mood lightened as she heard feet pounding down the interior stairway and a voice call out, "Jeez, Snickers. Give it a rest. It's just Terri."

Between Jen's voice and Snickers' greeting, Terri thought she just might make it through the evening after all. She accepted a warm welcome home hug and kiss from Jen. Jen's smile was hopeful, but faded quickly as she stepped back to survey Terri's face. "Bad day, baby?"

Terri nodded. "Not the best, that's for sure."

Jen's brows knitted and her mouth quirked into a crooked pout. "Can I assume that the visit to the therapist didn't go as planned?"

"You could say that."

"Oh, shit. Are you still on restriction?"

"Yes, I'm still officially a loose cannon with questionable judgment for at least two more weeks. I don't know what to say to these people to convince them that I can work."

Jen pulled her close, offering another hug and a quick kiss. "Baby, we'll figure this out. Why don't you head upstairs to change? Maybe a quick shower will make you feel better, and

I'll get us a glass of wine. Sound good?"

"Actually, that sounds perfect." Terri leaned in, giving Jen a quick kiss in return. "Thanks, sweetie."

Terri entered the bedroom, headed straight to her dresser, and performed the nightly ritual of securing her basically unused weapon in the top drawer. Her hands moved automatically, but she couldn't stop wondering if she would ever look at her weapon the same way again. Terri stripped out of her work clothes quickly and took a moment to stare at her reflection in the mirror. She noted that she did look tired, but decided it would probably be cured by ten minutes of hot water followed by a chilled glass of wine. That did sound better than hanging around, feeling sorry for herself. Maybe dinner out would be a nice addition to the evening, too. Terri allowed that thought to drift off as she turned the handles for the shower. Letting the hot spray of the water work out the kinks in her neck, she began to relax. A light tapping on the door brought her back to awareness as Jen gently pushed the door open.

"Baby, I left your wine on the nightstand. I have to run upstairs to shut down a program I was working on for school. I'll be back down in five minutes, okay?"

"That's fine, sweetie. Take your time." Terri heard the door click shut as she relaxed back into the hot water. "Why can't it all be this easy? It used to be."

After taking a moment to soap up and rinse, she twisted the handles to shut off the water and grabbed a towel to dry off. Terri felt a little of the day's disappointment drain away. She slipped into her white terrycloth bathrobe, headed for the nightstand, and grabbed her glass of wine. She got as far as sitting down on the side of the bed, when Jen returned, asking,

"Better, now?"

"Probably as good as it's going to get for tonight anyway."

A flirty smile appeared on Jen's face as she leaned against the doorframe with her arms crossed over her chest. "I bet I can make you forget about your lousy day."

"And just how are you going to do that? Erase my memory?"

"Aw, baby, I don't think so. That's just cheesy crap that they do on TV. I have a much more effective solution in mind." Jen came closer, stopping between Terri's knees, pulled at the front of the bathrobe with both hands, and knelt to plant little kisses up and down Terri's neck.

Terri relaxed into the attention being lavished on her neck, allowing her head to roll to the side, granting better access to Jen's ministrations. "Mmmm, that is a better idea."

Jen answered, voice muffled by terrycloth and Terri's neck. "I thought you might like it."

"You thought I might like it? I think you knew that I might like it." She pulled Jen up from her knees, urging her to lie on top, pinning Terri to the bed. "I think you knew that I would definitely like it." Terri kissed Jen soundly from below, and trailed her hands down Jen's back before gently placing hands on denim-clad hips, pulling her closer. "But I definitely would like it more"—Terri tugged on the pockets of the jeans for emphasis—"if these were gone."

Jen rolled over and jumped up, eager to comply. "I can do that." She used the toe of one shoe to remove the other by heel as she undid the buttons of her jeans. Jen removed the remaining shoe and shimmied out of her pants. Before she could jump back on the bed, Terri stopped her with a gentle foot to the abdomen.

"While you're up, why don't you take care of that pesky

T-shirt, too?" Terri bit her lip, watching intently as Jen peeled off her T-shirt. Terri moved her foot enough to allow the shirt to come off, and then put her foot back, stopping Jen. "Just get naked, all right?" Jen again eagerly complied, removing her socks, bra, and underpants. She jumped back on the bed, following Terri on all fours as Terri scooted higher on the bed.

Terri relaxed as Jen once again pinned her to the bed, pulling her bathrobe open, allowing naked bodies to touch. "See, I was right. That is better."

Jen purred her agreement, returning with little kisses and bites to Terri's neck and collarbones. While Jen's attentions were delightful, Terri found that she couldn't concentrate, as her thoughts seemed determined to drift back to her conversation with the therapist. The thought of two more weeks in limbo warred with the pleasure she felt as Jen's attentive mouth explored, seeking out and finding first one nipple, then the other, and Terri's own hands found their way to Jen's cute little butt. Using her hands and legs to apply not-so-gentle pressure, Terri urged Jen forward, attempting to telegraph her need for friction. Jen obliged, grinding herself into Terri's ever-dampening pussy. "That's it." Terri arched into the contact. "That's right." Her words degraded into a simple moan, as she used the pleasurable feeling to push aside the remnants of her own self-doubt.

As nice as the rocking and grinding were, Terri needed more. Jen dropped her head to nibble on Terri's neck. Terri's hot breath in her ear voiced a request.

"Touch me, Jen... please."

Jen shifted to straddle Terri's right leg, grinding her own wet pussy into Terri's muscular thigh, drawing a long moan from both women, as Jen's hand found its way to soft brunette curls, dampened with desire. Terri again attempted to reach for the contact, arching her hips in encouragement, rewarded with the feeling of gentle fingers urging her open, begging for entrance. The fingers began to stroke, long, loving strokes through the ample wetness.

"Want more, baby?"

The question, not to mention the presence of Jen's fingers, stoked Terri's fire even further, as she struggled to answer between ragged breaths. "Yes...please...I want you inside."

"Do you want me to fuck you?"

"Oh, God, yes. Fuck me slow. Take your time." The fingers finally slid home, two of them, Terri arching as much as she could against the fingers and Jen who straddled her leg. As good as this felt, it still wasn't enough. She struggled to voice her request, as the fingers began a slow in and out motion. "More... please...I need more of you."

She seemed aware that it was not the time for teasing, so Jen complied, adding a third finger with her next inward plunge. Terri moaned her appreciation loudly and dug her short fingernails into Jen's back, encouraging her actions, as Jen asked another question. "Is that better?"

"Oh, yes."

As the outside world finally began to slip away, Terri focused on the feeling of the fingers in her pussy and the hot voice in her ear asking another question. "Harder?"

"Please."

As the tempo and intensity increased, Terri's ability to speak decreased, reduced to a series of groans and other unintelligible sounds.

"Is that good, baby? Is that what you like?"

Terri responded the only way she had left. Moaning loudly, she arched into the sensation, moving in perfect synch with Jen's fingers. She felt the first tickle in her lower back, increasing her own movement to match, alerting Jen to the impending climax.

"Are you going to come for me, baby? Tell me about it. Tell the neighborhood."

Jen's words finally allowed the dam to break, as Terri announced, as requested, to anyone within earshot, with a sound that could only be described as a cross between a scream and a growl. As she relaxed from the intense orgasm, a second dam broke. Her body wracked by broken sobs, Terri wept as the intense negativity of the day was finally released. She pulled Jen into a needy hug, desperate for the release, as well as the closeness of someone she loved so much. Jen held her, allowing the emotions to run their course, before she reclaimed her fingers and stroked away the tears streaming down Terri's face.

"Terri, baby, what's wrong? Did I hurt you?"

Terri looked deeply into Jen's beautiful green eyes, attempting to piece together her shattered emotions.

"Sorry, sweetie, just a bad day." She pulled Jen close for another bone-crunching hug. "I'm so worried all the time that I can't do this. I can't be what you need. I can't be what anyone needs."

Jen pulled back to reestablish eye contact. "I need you. Just you."

"Do you, Jen? Do you really? I'm not exactly what you fell in love with right now."

"Terri, of course I need you. I wish I knew what to say to really make you believe that." Jen slid over so Terri could roll onto her side and arrange herself more comfortably on the bed.

"We've talked about this before. I'm happier than I've ever been in my life, and that's all because of you. Please believe me."

"I know. It's just, well, you know..." Terri searched for understanding in Jen's face. "It's just hard for me. Everything is so different, and I'm so happy that you're here, but it's just strange."

"Baby, it's different for both of us, but it's so worth it. I know I came charging in here with my crazy dog and enough computer hardware to make your beautiful studio look like Mission Control in Houston, but I want you. I want to be as close to you as possible. I was really starting to hate Sunday evenings, because it meant that I had to leave. Now I don't, and right here is the only place in the world that I really want to be. That means I need you." Terri started to interrupt, but Jen stopped her with a finger to her lips. "I need you...not to protect me, but just to be with me."

As much as Terri hated the need to be reassured once again, Jen's words always managed to bring her back from the dark place. She finally allowed a small smile, making special note of how cute Jen was at the moment, lying on her tummy, leaning forward on her elbows, as one foot played mindlessly with the other. Terri scooted a little closer, placing a protective hand on Jen's back, rewarded with the soft feel of skin as Jen lowered her head and snuggled into the touch. "You really need me?"

Jen squirmed, answering with a soft "um-hum," as the hand on her back slid lower to become the hand on her butt. Knowing exactly what Jen needed, Terri shifted enough to remove the robe that had somehow remained magically attached to her arms through Jen's earlier attentions, tossing it to the end of the bed, returning her hand to Jen's beautiful backside. They both snuggled closer together as Terri tossed her leg across, effectively pinning Jen to the bed.

"So, what is it that you need?"

Answering with a soft moan, Jen attempted to telegraph her specific need, pressing the full length of her slight frame against Terri's more solid one. Terri's hand wandered up and down the freckled back as she attempted to coax the words out.

"That's a pretty vague answer, Dr. Rosenberg. I need more than that to work with."

She smiled a little as the body that was now pinned to the bed beneath her wordlessly begged for attention and Jen attempted to formulate an answer. "I need you to touch me."

"But I am touching you." Terri rolled to straddle Jen's leg, as she moved pillows aside, shooting an evil glance over her shoulder on the way. The evil glance softened to a look of delight as Terri moved her leg to apply just enough pressure to move Jen's legs a little farther apart. The resulting warmth against her own pussy distracted Terri for a moment, but she quickly returned to exploring Jen's soft skin.

"I mean, there's lots of ways that I can touch you." Terri reclaimed her hand, moving it up to push the auburn hair from Jen's neck. "I can do this..." She deposited a couple of well-placed kisses to her neck, and moved up to nibble on the closest earlobe. The resultant moan urged her on, as she continued to whisper between kisses and nibbles. "I know you like this." Terri pushed her breasts deliberately into Jen's back. "I know you like this, too. You like it when you can feel how hard my nipples are, pressed against you like this."

Jen seemed to be struggling to keep up her end of the conversation. "Oh God, Terri. You know I do." She squirmed a little more as the hand returned to her backside, this time stroking down the backs of her legs, drifting closer to the abundant wetness and heat that was now pouring out of her.

Terri knew that there was just so much teasing that Jen would take. "So, sweetie, tell me. Do you need me?"

Another moan, louder this time, one that sounded like arousal mixed with frustration. "Yes, Terri, I need you. I need you now."

"What do you need? Tell me." Terri teased, stroking closer and closer to the source of the heat. Jen struggled to answer between ragged breaths.

"Oh, shit. Terri. I need your fingers. I need to feel you slide into me."

Time to end the teasing. Terri slid her fingers closer to the heat, feeling the dampness as she explored Jen's opening, getting up on her knees to allow room for movement, but staying close enough to maintain the intimacy of the conversation. She slipped two fingers in easily as Jen groaned and arched back, forcing the fingers in as far as they would go. "Is that what you need, Jen?"

"Mmmm, yeah. That's it." Jen rocked back against the fingers as they were pulled out and pushed back in, slightly harder than the first time. "Do that again."

Terri complied, establishing a slow rhythm that she knew Jen would like. Jen responded, grinding back against each thrust, grabbing the top of the comforter with her fists so she could use her arms for leverage.

"Do you need more?"

"Yes... please... more..."

Strong muscles pulled her fingers deeper with each stroke,

and Terri could feel her own wetness bathing the back of Jen's thigh as each thrust forced Jen's leg firmly into her center. Terri added a third finger, and Jen moaned her appreciation loudly.

"Can you feel me on your leg? Can you feel how wet you make me?" Terri asked.

Jen's language skills were quickly disappearing, replaced by a collection of grunts and groans that Terri could only assume were answers to her questions. She tried another one, this one guaranteed to drive Jen completely wild. "Do you want me to touch myself while I fuck you?"

"Yes..." Jen forced an answer out through her clenched jaws, rocking back harder against the fingers in her pussy. "Oh God, yes."

Before she moved to comply, Terri asked one more question. "Can you do that for me too? Touch yourself... help me make you come?"

Jen didn't answer the question, as she moved to do as requested, sliding one hand under her body, seeking out her own swollen clit as Terri rocked back on her heels and moved her hand to do the same. The need for any further words tumbled away as Terri watched her hands, one in Jen's hot pussy, the other playing with her own. She could tell from the increased flow of wetness and Jen's more urgent movement, that she was close to release, and Terri knew that she was right there with her. She met each backward thrust of Jen's hips with a counterthrust of her own, pushing Jen and herself nearer to release. "Are you going to come, sweetie? Come all over my hand while I come on your leg?"

Terri's words and actions threw Jen over the edge, loudly crying out her release as a fresh gush of wetness coated

Terri's hand, and pulled her fingers in just a little more. Those sensations, combined with the action of her hand on her own clit, brought Terri to climax right behind Jen. She collapsed onto the bed, covering half of Jen with her own sweaty body. As their breathing slowed to a more normal speed and Terri reclaimed her fingers, the body beneath her began to shake with laughter. "What's so funny?"

"Sorry, baby. Just me being silly. I'm completely, stupidly happy, I'm madly in love, and I'm so totally well-fucked right now that life is just bliss. Hence the laughter. Tell me you feel better, baby."

"Yes, I do. Thank you."

"Ahhh, pfft. My pleasure...really." Jen was interrupted by a low growl in the pit of her stomach.

"Hungry, sweetie?"

"Evidently." Jen rolled over on her back and rubbed her tummy. "I could make us dinner."

Terri sat up to grab her cell phone from the pocket of her slacks, still draped across the foot of the bed, albeit not as neatly as when she had put them there. She tossed the phone to Jen. "Or, you could call Thai Chef. They're on speed dial."

"Ooh, good plan, Agent McKinnon." Jen made the call, ordering their usual. She snapped the phone closed. "They'll be here in forty-five minutes. What do you want to do until then?"

A leer and waggle of the eyebrows offered Terri's suggestion of the best way to kill three-quarters of an hour. Jen returned both leer and eyebrow waggle and tossed the phone back toward the foot of the bed.

CHAPTER SIX

Ow, ow, ow... hot!"

Denny wrestled with the pan of ramen noodles, trying unsuccessfully not to spill the boiling chicken broth as she poured it from the saucepan into a chipped cereal bowl. She took her dinner and headed for the small living space in her studio apartment. She set the hot soup on the wooden cable spool that served as both coffee table and work space, flipped open the cover of her laptop and pressed the power button.

After she flopped unceremoniously onto the worn futon that served as both sofa and bed, she pulled the computer onto her lap and checked to see who was online. Although she enjoyed the new city and school, she missed her friends at James Madison and always loved to hear the gossip about who was hooking up with whom, and which professors were making someone's life a living hell. Strangely enough, there was only one person online. She double-clicked on the name of an old buddy from both the softball team and the Information Systems Department, CLCheshire, and typed in a greeting.

AUHackrGrrrl: Hey girl!

CLCheshire: Hey backatcha! Wassup?

AUHackrGrrrl: Nada...dinner break. You?

CLCheshire: same here. How's grad school?

AUHackrGrrrl: Great, challenging, busy...good stuff. How's life at the ISAT building?

CLCheshire: same again. Sucks that you got to keep Dr. Rosenberg. Don't like the new guy. Piles of work.

AUHackrGrrrl: Yeah, I did all right with that. She's even cooler than we thought.

CLCheshire: Oh, do tell!

AUHackrGrrrl: Well, all of our speculation about her being queer was right.

CLCheshire: No shit! Not terribly surprised.

AUHackrGrrrl: Yeah, me neither. I busted her making out in the alley with her g/f last weekend.

CLCheshire: lol :-)

AUHackrGrrrl: Can you stand it?

CLCheshire: That's pretty cool.

AUHackrGrrrl: Yeah, I thought so. I got to meet the g/f.

CLCheshire: and...

AUHackrGrrrl: And she's like this totally hot FBI agent.

CLCheshire: Again, I say no shit.

AUHackrGrrrl: No shit...she seemed really cool.

CLCheshire: Well, good for Dr. R.

AUHackrGrrrl: Yeah, I said the same thing to her.

CLCheshire: You did not!

AUHackrGrrrl: Yeah, kind of slipped out. oops

CLCheshire: You were never good at the thinking before speaking thing.

AUHackrGrrrl: Nothing's changed.

AUHackrGrrrl: Oh, oh... there's more!

CLCheshire: What?

AUHackrGrrrl: Remember last year. Right before spring break when she got so weird.

CLCheshire: Yeah?

AUHackrGrrrl: Dude, this crazy guy showed up at her house and tried to kill her.

CLCheshire: WTF?

AUHackrGrrrl: No, really. She told me about it. Put a gun to her head and threatened to blow her brains out.

CLCheshire: Explains a lot.

AUHackrGrrrl: Doesn't it. That's how she met the hot FBI agent.

CLCheshire: Aw, man. Not a great way to meet girls.

AUHackrGrrrl: lol...she said the same thing to me.

CLCheshire: Why did she tell you all this?

AUHackrGrrrl: I got a strange call about a job. Hacking for cash. I asked her about it.

CLCheshire: yeah?

AUHackrGrrrl: Yeah...she told me that she did that in school and the crazy mofo that tried to kill her had something to do with it.

CLCheshire: So what about the job? Gonna take it?

AUHackrGrrrl: Don't know. I really need the cash.

CLCheshire: Are you worried about it?

AUHackrGrrrl: Nah... what's the chance of that happening again? Like getting struck by lightning.

CLCheshire: That would suck... but so does being broke.

AUHackrGrrrl: Like you'd know. How's that new car

from Daddy?

CLCheshire: err, um...nice, red, fast. I know....

AUHackrGrrrl: No worries... just kidding.

CLCheshire: s'cool.

AUHackrGrrrl: Just me talking before I think again.

CLCheshire: No problem. Still doesn't answer my question.

AUHackrGrrrl: Which one?

CLCheshire: Scroll up... gonna take the job?

AUHackrGrrrl: Probably. I'll decide when the person calls back. The money might be too good to pass up.

CLCheshire: Sounds like a plan.

AUHackrGrrrl: hang on...phone

CLCheshire: ok

Denny sat back to retrieve her cell phone. She checked the caller ID, noting that it was the same number that the job offer had come from. She flipped the phone open and answered.

"Hello?"

The voice on the other end of the call sounded confident and perhaps a little sultry. Decidedly female. "Denise Robertson?"

Denny hesitated just long enough to process that the voice didn't match the first call that she'd received from the same phone number. "Yes, this is Denise."

"Well, Ms. Robertson...Denise. Do you prefer Denise?"

"Actually, most everyone calls me Denny."

The voice was smooth, like silk, maybe a little bit of an edge. Attitude perhaps. "Well then, Denny it is. My boss wanted me to give you a call. Have you had a chance to think about his offer?"

Denny struggled against her trepidation to answer the question. "Honestly, the whole thing makes me a little nervous."

Denny heard a small chuckle on the other end of the call. "Would a little more money cure those nerves? The original offer was thirty-five hundred dollars. Right?"

"Umm, yeah. That's right."

"Would seventy-five hundred help with the jitters?"

"Umm, wow. Umm, probably." Denny's mouth quirked into a crooked smile, still unsure, but that was a lot of money. She looked at the cooling bowl of soup, and quickly came to the realization that seventy-five hundred dollars would nicely remove her from the I'm-so-poor-that-I-have-to-eat-ramen-noodles club. She was okay with that, despite her trepidation. The smooth voice brought her back to earth.

"So, Denny. Can we put you on the payroll?"

Denny exhaled loudly and steeled her resolve. "Yes... count me in."

The voice brightened. "Rockin' good choice, Denny. Welcome aboard! I'll bring the paperwork by your apartment in a little while. I can't wait to meet you."

The nerves were back. "Umm, ok. You too. Do you need the address?"

"No, thanks. I'm good. Later."

Before she could ask for a name or description, the call was terminated on the other end. Denny set the phone on the cable spool next to the computer, all the while wondering if what she had just agreed to had been a mistake. The call jarred her nerves to the point that she almost forgot about her friend online. She woke her laptop and got back to the conversation.

AUHackrGrrrl: back.... Sorry about that. It was someone about that job.

CLCheshire: Well?

AUHackrGrrrl: Well, they offered me more money, so I said I'd do it.

CLCheshire: Are you sure about this?

AUHackrGrrrl: What's gonna happen?

CLCheshire: Yeah, you're probably right. Gonna tell Dr. R. about it?

AUHackrGrrrl: Nope... she made her feelings clear. It'll be fine

CLCheshire: Good plan. She's kind of high-strung anyway.

AUHackrGrrrl: Yeah, someone's on the way with some info, so I need to go. Later?

CLCheshire: ok...Later :-)

CLCheshire has signed off.

Denny started to fold down the screen of her laptop, but changed her mind as she wondered if she'd need it for the impending conversation with the mystery caller. Cloak and dagger or not, Denny just couldn't turn down seventy-five hundred bucks. A few minutes later, the door buzzer sounded. "Wow, that was quick," she said into the air. As she opened the door, the first thing she saw was a worn pair of motorcycle boots leading up to the tightest pair of black leather pants that she'd ever seen. Any attempt at not staring was lost as her gaze traveled upward, over a more-than-snug black tank top with ample cleavage spilling over the low neckline, and short black leather jacket. Denny's mouth dropped slightly open as she met the dark brown eyes of the stranger. Speech was gone, replaced by a sense of wonder. Holy shit... she was gorgeous. The stranger shifted the envelope filled with paperwork to her left hand, offering up her right one in greeting.

"Hi, you must be Denny. I'm Faith."

After a failed attempt to say hello, Denny cleared her throat and finally squeaked out a greeting. "Hi. Yeah... Denny... that's right." She finally remembered her manners enough to shake the offered hand, releasing it to invite Faith into her apartment. "Come on in."

"Thanks. I can't stay long." After stepping into the room enough to close the door behind her, Faith tossed the envelope on the cable spool in the middle of the room and pointed toward it. "All the info you need for the job is in there. There's also a little down payment for your trouble. Look it over tonight, and if you have any questions, give me a call." Denny looked at the envelope, but quickly returned her gaze to Faith, who was now looking her up and down with an almost feral glint in her eye.

"Okay, I'll do that."

Faith smiled. Actually, Faith leered at Denny. "So are you a real skater boi, or do you just dress like one?"

Denny realized that she was being cruised, and kind of enjoyed the sensation, despite the fact that she was also struggling against feeling like a scared shitless thirteen-year-old. She looked down at her clothing. Baggy cargo shorts with boxers peeking over the waistband, loose sweatshirt, a ratty pair of Vans skater shoes, and her old JMU baseball cap turned backward over her short haircut. "Umm, no. I don't do the skater thing. I was a shortstop at JMU....softball, you know."

"Softball, huh? That's cool." Denny could only watch as

Faith stepped forward, closing the gap between them. "I think we're going to work well together; don't you?"

The only thing Denny's brain was capable of piecing together was, "Holy shit, look at those tits!" Fortunately, she was able to keep the comment to herself as she took a breath in an attempt to compose herself and tried to come up with something more meaningful to say. All that came out was, "Umm, yeah. Work. Okay."

Faith licked her lips and, motioned toward the envelope with her chin. "Why don't you get started on that? I'll call you in a couple of days and see what's up."

"Umm, sure. Okay."

Smooth, Denny. Real smooth.

Faith moved closer again, this time forcing Denny to choose either to step back or face the tantalizing prospect of those magnificent tits smooshed up against her own under the soft fleece of her sweatshirt. Choosing the more chivalrous option, Denny stepped back, knocked the backs of her legs against the futon, and sat down hard. Actually, she fell down, but made a show of nonchalance that she hoped didn't make her look like too much of a dork. Evidently, it worked as Faith stepped back and spoke.

"You're cute. Maybe we'll need to go out for a drink next time we talk."

Oh, shit. Gulp again. "Sure," she squeaked out, cleared her throat, and repeated the word, with much better effect this time. "Sure. That'd be great."

"Yeah, I thought you might think so." Faith turned to leave, swinging her hips around in a manner that forced Denny to lock on to the fine, leather-clad butt that was right at eye level from her seat on the futon. Faith pulled the door open and left the apartment with a quick, "See ya, D."

All Denny could do was continue to stare, open-mouthed, as the door closed, cutting off the gorgeous ass from her sight. As the bolt clicked shut, she shook her head and smacked herself on the forehead with the palm of her hand. "Jeez, you're a dork!" Denny finally collected herself enough to turn her attention to the envelope sitting on the cable spool next to the computer. "So what do we have here?"

***

Faith made her way slowly down the steps of the converted townhouse into the early evening darkness of the Tenleytown section of DC. Whistling as she hit the sidewalk, she turned and headed toward her motorcycle parked around the corner. Once she was sure that she was out of sight and earshot of the hacker's apartment, she pulled her cell phone out of the inside pocket of her leather jacket and made a call. She didn't have to wait long for an answer.

"Any problems?"

"No, sir. She was eating out of my hand in seconds." Faith cradled the phone between her ear and shoulder as she rooted in her jacket pocket for a crumpled pack of smokes. She pulled the last one free with her lips, lit the cigarette with a Zippo lighter, crumpled the empty pack, and tossed it into a nearby planter.

"I knew you were the right person for this job. Let's just say I've heard really positive things about your particular skill set."

"Thanks. I don't think we'll have any problems with Little

Miss Skater Boi."

"You didn't scare her, did you, Faith?"

"Well, maybe a little, but isn't that part of the skill set that you hired me for?"

"Yes, it is. Just don't break her."

"No, sir. She might be quaking in her sneakers, but I promise she'll be back for more. Consider it done."

"I knew I could count on you. Call in tomorrow, and we'll discuss what happens next. Thank you, Faith."

Faith drew heavily on her cigarette. "Yes, sir." She snapped the phone closed and returned it to its pocket as she blew smoke into the lightly chilled fall night air. A quick flick of her fingers and the still-burning butt flew into the street. Faith climbed on the motorcycle and pulled a black helmet on over her head. A turn of a key gunned the bike to life. She knocked the kickstand up with her booted left foot, twisted the gas with her right hand, and released the clutch with her left, roaring off down the quiet side street and back into the lights and traffic of the nation's capital.

Mission accomplished.

CHAPTER SEVEN

Jen woke up and attempted to shake off her confusion at the fact that it was still dark in the house. It didn't take long to realize why she was awake as Terri thrashed lightly next to her, pulling at the sheets, murmuring the word "no" over and over again, like a mantra. Nightmare again. Jen immediately shook off the cobwebs and rolled over to prop herself on one elbow to try to calm Terri from what Jen knew were horrific images.

"Baby, shhh. Wake up."

Terri continued to thrash, pulling harder at the sheet as it quickly became soaked with cold sweat. The nightmares had become less frequent, but Jen knew she had to act quickly to pull Terri out of the clutches of the frightening dream.

"Terri! Wake up!"

The words apparently reached Terri as she startled awake, sat bolt upright in the bed, and shouted, "No!" She looked around the room, wide-eyed, obviously confused by her surroundings and the partially moonlit darkness of the house. Jen sat up fully and rubbed small circles on Terri's quivering back, hoping her touch would calm the shakes.

"Baby, I'm here. It's just a dream."

Terri looked at her, confused in the semi-darkness, searching for understanding. Jen watched her face as realization began to dawn. "That's right. Just a dream. You're okay now."

Terri slowly rubbed her face with both hands, but her body would not stop shaking. "You're okay, Jen?"

"I'm fine, baby. All kinds of fine here." Jen smiled, sliding her hand up to Terri's neck, kneading lightly at the knotted muscles there. She could feel the change as Terri's breathing slowed to a more normal rate "You're okay too. I promise. Nothing bad happened." Jen used her free arm to wrap around the front of Terri and pulled her into a comforting sideways hug. Terri nestled into the embrace, welcoming the comfort that had become such a habit over the past several months. Jen lay back against the pillow, her arm still wrapped around Terri. She tucked Terri's head in under her chin and lightly kissed the top of her head. "Do you want to tell me about it?"

"No, I don't think so."

Jen hugged her closer and urged her to reconsider, "I think it would help."

"What makes you think that?" Terri pulled back and disentangled herself from Jen's embrace.

Jen bit her lip. She had to fight the urge to let it go like she usually did. She wanted desperately to see the worry lines on Terri's face disappear, but she knew the discussion had to happen sooner or later.

"Because you don't talk about it, and you're still having nightmares. Why won't you let me help?"

Terri sat up and met Jen's gaze with one that was almost

defiant. "Because this is something I need to fix."

Well, it was out there now, and Jen figured she had nothing to lose by pushing. "How are you going to fix this by yourself? It doesn't seem to me that the patented Agent McKinnon stoicism is working. Please, Terri, let me help you."

Terri's lips pressed into a thin line and her nostrils flared as she took a deep, slow breath. Jen cringed as she realized the expression on Terri's face was one she hadn't seen before... anger.

"So, the brilliant Dr. Rosenberg has all the answers now. Great. That's just fucking great. Thank you so much."

Jen recoiled, shocked by Terri's harsh tone of voice. "No, no... that's not what I meant." She reached out, once again offering comfort, but Terri shied away from the touch, and pulled her knees up to hug them against her chest. "Baby, please..."

"What?" Terri shot back through clenched teeth.

"Please, let's not do this. I really do want to help. Please, it's Sunday morning and we don't have to get up for anything. Let's go downstairs. I'll make us some tea, and we can talk."

Terri appeared to relax a little at the suggestion, visibly lowering her shoulders. Jen could see that she was still guarding. Terri still had her arms wrapped around her knees, but any sign that Terri might let her in was welcome.

"Okay...maybe you're right. That might be a good idea."

Jen sat up and swung her feet over the side of the bed while Terri headed for the bathroom.

"Go on and start the water for the tea, Jen. I just need a second here."

Jen listened as the bathroom door clicked shut and the water came on. She padded barefoot down the steps and into the kitchen, stopping long enough to light a candle on the counter; soft light seemed the best option for fragile nerves. She put the kettle on and took two mugs out of the cabinet.

When she heard the unmistakable sound of toenails on hardwood, Jen turned to see Snickers standing by his food bowl and yawning, apparently wondering why people were up so early. She sat on the floor, cross-legged, and patted her lap, urging her muttly little friend to come sit with her. "Hey, buddy." She skritched behind his ears and thumped him on the back as he attempted to wiggle into the nest of her crossed legs. Soft footfalls on the steps alerted her to Terri's arrival, but she stayed on the floor with Snickers.

"You two look comfy."

Jen looked up at Terri in the soft light. Wrapped in a robe, with wet hair and dark circles under her eyes, she didn't look like a badass FBI agent. She looked vulnerable, almost fragile.

"We're good, aren't we, Snickers?" After a couple more well placed pats to the dog's flanks, Jen looked up. "What about you, baby? Are you better now?"

Terri sat on the floor with her back against the stove next to Jen. "I'm pretty sure I'm not going to bite your head off again, if that's what you mean by better."

Jen laughed. "That's good." She smiled when Terri reached over to squeeze her hand.

"I'm really sorry, sweetie. What I said was totally uncalled for."

Jen waved it off. "It's okay. I've never really pushed that hard before, and it probably caught you off guard. I'm sorry if it pissed you off."

"Well, it did piss me off."

Jen stiffened but relaxed as she felt her hand squeezed again.

"But while I was in the bathroom, I realized that I wasn't pissed at you. I guess I'm really angry with myself. I've let this thing brew because I didn't want to trouble you with it. I'm just used to dealing with everything alone, and I'm not always sure how to open up."

"I'm sure the nightmares don't help."

"No, they don't. I know we haven't talked about it much, but it's tough to watch someone you love as much as I love you get their brains splattered all over the wall night after night and still trust that they're going to be here tomorrow. So yeah, I stuff a lot of things that bother me."

Jen turned her attention from the hand that was holding hers to Terri's sad eyes. It hurt to see someone she loved in so much pain. "Baby, I'm not going anywhere. Is that what you're worried about?"

"Honestly, Jen, yes. I came so close to losing you that I get scared. And there are some other things that I've just never asked about."

"Things? What things?"

The look on Terri's face told Jen that she was having difficulty with the answer. "Baby, whatever it is, you can say it."

"I know. Well, maybe I don't or I would have said something before. This is going to sound stupid—"

Jen stopped that thought with a hand to Terri's chin, pulling her face up to make eye contact. "Terri, listen to me. If it bothers you this much, it's not stupid. Please tell me what's wrong."

"It's something that happened a long time ago, and I should have said something earlier. Do you remember last winter? The phone call from Davis?"

Jen shuddered. She definitely remembered the phone call from the man who tried to kill her. "You said he called you at work and made a lot of noise about stuff just to mess with your head. You never told me exactly what he said."

"He did make a lot of noise, mostly about things you'd done in the past. I ignored it at the time, and then everything happened, and I got hurt, and then you weren't here, and now you are, so I just let it go. Maybe I didn't really let it go. He said some hateful stuff about you."

"What did he say?" Terri once again seemed hesitant, so Jen pushed some more. "Terri, you have to tell me. I need to know what he said so I can try to fix it. It might not be true."

"God, this is hard." Terri hesitated for just a second before plowing ahead. "Jen, he accused you of some things. I don't want to believe it, but I need to know. He said you were involved in some illegal computer stuff. Was that true?"

Jen nodded. "Since we're doing the big honesty thing here, I have to say yes. But before you freak out, it was only a couple of times, and I would never do it again."

"Jen, what did you do?"

Jen considered and rejected several options to explain her actions. She opted again for the honest approach. "Okay... the Weasel taught me how to hack into banks. I did that a few times." She stopped, allowing the words to sink in. "But I never stole anything. It was kind of a rush just to be able to get in. That's big stuff to a nineteen-year-old kid."

"I suppose."

"The worst thing I did was I hacked into the university intranet and—"

"And what?"

"I'm sorry, Terri. This is really hard."

"Jen, what did you do?"

Jen cringed. She knew the answer wasn't something that her honest-to-a-fault FBI agent would like. "I made a deal with some people to hack into the system and change their grades."

"What kind of a deal did you make with these people?"

Well, it was out there now. "They offered me money. I was always broke, so I took it."

Terri said nothing. She got up, pulling her hand away as Jen reached for it. "I'm really sorry, but it was a long time ago. I know it was wrong. Can't we just chalk it up to me being a stupid kid?" She reached for Terri's hand one more time, and again met with nothing but air.

"Just give me a minute. What kind of tea do you want?"

Jen began inwardly kicking herself. Maybe complete disclosure wasn't the right option. "Whatever you're having. I really don't care."

Terri again said nothing as she reached over the stove to the cupboard with the tea. Jen watched from her spot on the floor as Terri pulled down the box of vanilla almond, holding it out for approval. Jen nodded and returned her attention to Snickers' ears while Terri dropped the teabags into the mugs on the counter and then poured water over them. She sat back down next to Jen and took her hand.

"That's pretty bad stuff, you know?"

Jen was still feeling about an inch tall, but was comforted by the warmth of Terri's hand surrounding her own. "I know, baby. It was really stupid. I could have gotten tossed out of school, or worse."

"That's fraud, and it's a felony offense. You could have gotten arrested. It's good that there's such a thing as statute of limitations, or you could still be liable for your actions."

"Are you going to handcuff me and turn me in, Agent McKinnon?"

"Sweetie, this isn't funny. Besides, I think you'd enjoy the cuffs, and that's off topic. You broke the law in a big way. I know I haven't been much of one lately, but I'm still a cop. I have to let it go, but you'll understand that it makes me worry."

Jen pushed Snickers out of her lap so she could turn, getting on her knees in front of Terri. "Baby, I know it was wrong and I can promise you that I'll never do anything like that again. You have to believe me. I know it would make a mess for you, and I seriously learned my lesson about the time Davis was holding a gun to my head." She hesitated while Terri shuddered, evidently recalling her earlier nightmare. "I have lots of incentive to behave myself now. Promise. Besides, Denny was in my office just last week asking about the same thing." She hesitated again as a puzzled expression crossed Terri's features. "Someone called her about a job. It sounded like one of those hacking for cash deals. I told her in no uncertain terms that it was a bad idea, and I'm pretty sure she listened to me."

"I hope she did. We're busting people right and left for that exact same thing. It's a huge problem. But I do believe you when you say you won't do it again. I've never had my life threatened by a lunatic hacker from my past, but I've been pretty close to it. That would make me behave—"

"Same here. Trust me, baby. Never again."

"I do trust you."

Jen finally felt the tension in the room recede. As she

leaned forward to offer a hug, she remembered something else. "Baby?" She sat back on her heels, once again taking Terri's hands in her own.

"Hmmm?"

"You said that he said a couple of things to you. While we're still on the honesty train here, what was the other thing?"

"Well, actually, he might have mentioned something else. He asked me if you hit on me. He kind of suggested that you might have been working me romantically just for the protection of the FBI."

Jen sat back on her heels as her mouth dropped open in shock. "That asshole! I can't believe that he said that. Terri, I've been completely honest with you about all of that stuff. Granted, when I was younger, I had a little trouble keeping my pants zipped, especially if there were softball players involved, and there was that one time, well, two times, at the Women's Final Four, but..." She waved a hand in the air to dispel her own musing, "So now, despite the appearance of my new graduate assistant, I am over that and only have eyes for one extremely hot blue-eyed cop. And I know she feels the same way about me. So, regardless of my history, I'm all yours now, whether you want me or not."

Jen pulled her close for another hug, then backed away to offer a long kiss, pushing aside the last wall that she had to hide behind. "Agent McKinnon, you are stuck with me. So please try to take some comfort from that. Okay?"

"Okay. I will."

"You'd better." Jen could plainly see that Terri was still thinking, so she urged her on. "Something else? I can see it all over your face."

"Women's Final Four, huh? You didn't tell me about that one."

"Not much to tell really. She was hot, and actually, she looked a lot like you." Jen stopped and attempted to revise her statement, quickly realizing that she was dangerously close to treading on thin ice, as evidenced by Terri's arched brow. "Well, not a lot like you. Just maybe sort of a little bit like you. With a limp. Oh, and I seem to remember now that she might have—"

"Jen, you can stop now."

Jen swiped the back of her hand across her forehead in an exaggerated fashion. "Whew, good. I was kind of digging a hole for myself there. But you're smiling now, so it's good, right?"

"Yeah, Jen, it's good."

Jen reached over Terri's head, grabbed both mugs, and offered one to Terri. "Here. Now drink your tea. It's getting cold. Do you want some breakfast?"

"Jen, sweetie, it's three thirty in the morning. How about if we just go back to bed?"

Jen stretched and yawned as full realization dawned that it was, in fact, still the middle of the night. "That sounds like a great idea."

CHAPTER EIGHT

Terri waited, bouncing lightly on her toes, shifting her weight from foot to foot. After a fourth obsessive check of her watch, she huffed and set her computer bag down. Bobby was late. But then again, that was really nothing new. As she was just about to give up waiting and call him, a large, gray, windowless panel van pulled into the driveway of the parking garage where she was standing. She huffed again, slightly agitated at being made to wait, pulled the passenger side door open, and climbed into the van. Shooting a quick, evil glance at Bobby in the driver's seat, she began to chastise him for his tardiness.

"You're late."

Bobby waved it off. "Sorry. You know me. I had to make myself pretty for you."

She laughed at the ridiculous notion. "Bobby, give it up."

Bobby grinned. "I have to try. No, really, the van wasn't ready. One of the video monitors was on the fritz, and I had to wait while they changed a cable. Forgive me now?"

"Only 'cause it's you." She slid her briefcase into the space between the front seats. "If I haven't already said this sixteen times, thanks for talking McNally into letting me come along. I know it's just surveillance, but at least I'm out of the office."

"Don't worry about it, kiddo. I figured you could use the break, and since Stansfield's wife just had her baby, I was able to help him out too. I know we both hate watch detail, but it is better than being stuck inside."

"Yes, and I really appreciate the support, even if I'm not officially allowed out of the truck. But you're right about one thing. I really hate surveillance."

"Oh, I don't know. Sitting in a dark van, drinking lukewarm coffee in the middle of the night... sounds like more fun than humans should be allowed to have, in my humble opinion. Beats the shit out of being cuddled up naked with a hot little college professor, right?"

Terri shot Bobby one more evil glance. "What makes you think that's where I'd be right now?"

"Girl, please. Don't even try to tell me that you'd be anywhere else right now. I know better than that."

"Just drive."

Bobby threw the transmission into drive and gunned the engine. "Yes, ma'am."

He drove the loop around the Lincoln Memorial and headed down to the warehouse district known as Southeast. Terri leaned the seat back and put both feet on the dashboard to relax for the half-hour drive. "Did you get any sleep?" Bobby asked. "We haven't done the night shift thing for a while."

"Yeah, I slept for a couple hours before Jen got home. She had a meeting tonight, so I curled up with Snickers for a little while. I'll be good with that. I'd be better if we could stop for coffee on the way."

"Consider it done." Bobby scanned the side of the road for an open 7-Eleven as he drove. Fifteen minutes and one brief stop later, they were rolling again toward one of the seedier sections of the nation's capital.

The ride passed in companionable silence. Terri really did hate surveillance duty. Monotonous hours spent watching nothing happen on a video monitor was not her idea of fun. Not to mention the lousy location and the almost ever-present lack of a bathroom. Not fun indeed. Well, at least she was outside and away from the sideways glances of the other agents in the shared space of the Hoover Building. Terri didn't relish being the "defective agent" on staff. It didn't sit well with her sense of order, and besides, she had specifically chosen this career field to provide a way for her to do some good in the world, not just take up space in an office. "At least I'm outside," she thought, a little more out loud than she realized. Loud enough to get Bobby's attention.

"What? Terri, did you say something?"

"Nothing... just thinking out loud."

"What about?"

"In all the years we've been working together, did you ever think you'd get to hear me say that I was happy to be in the truck?"

"Well, no, not really. I know you hate this, probably more than I do, but I thought you could use the break from the office. I also thought that maybe it might give us a chance to talk."

"Everyone wants me to talk about 'it'" Terri punctuated the word with air quotes. "Have I become so dark and enigmatic that people have to drag me out of, well, wherever I am to get me to talk about things?"

"Terri, you are someplace dark, and I suppose enigmatic is as good a word as any to describe your behavior lately. But I need you to hold that thought. We're here. Get the sheet out and help me find the place we're supposed to park."

Terri picked up her bag and began rooting through the case file to locate the map. She found it and began comparing the streets and building numbers on the map to the ones that were now just outside her window. "Here.... Bobby, slow down, this is it."

Bobby slowed the van, ducking to look under the rearview mirror as he did. "Yep, that's it." He pointed straight ahead. "Look, there's some construction vehicles over there. Looks like a good spot to spend the night."

Terri agreed, and Bobby pulled the panel van around the corner of the building, out of sight of the street, but close enough to the entrance that they could watch anyone coming or going. The van fit in nicely with the other vehicles scattered about. Two small surveillance cameras had been set up inside earlier by agents posing as warehouse workers, allowing a limited visual of the large interior space. Audio pickups accompanied the cameras, allowing equally limited access to any conversation that might take place as well. Terri quietly sighed to herself as she looked in the side mirror, noting the Porta-John twenty yards to the rear of the van. Good. Now she could finish her coffee in peace.

Bobby killed the engine, pulled out the keys, and dropped them into the pocket of his short black jacket. Terri slid her briefcase toward the back of the van as she climbed between the high-backed seats, working her way toward the cramped space in the back. She opened two folding chairs that had been bungeed to the side of the truck and took one, while Bobby maneuvered his much larger frame into the back, pulling the remaining chair over toward the small bank of monitors, recorders, and various other electronic paraphernalia. Terri settled herself in to organize her workspace. She pulled her laptop out of the depths of her briefcase and plugged into the power outlet next to the video recorder. She flipped open the top and pressed the power button, which brought the small computer to life. The wireless router in the van would allow her to access the FBI database, as well as full connection to the Internet, just in case. The sound of laughter to her right drew her attention from the computer screen.

"What's so funny, Agent Kraft?"

"I was just thinking that if you got really bored, you could always IM Jen for a little cyber nookie."

"Don't think so, Bobby. Besides, after that little misadventure with the radio last winter, you've had plenty of details. We're done with that now."

"Awww, meanie." Terri shot one last evil glance toward him. He waved her off. "Besides, how could you ever top the way you two were going at it on the kitchen table? Anything else, I fear, would be anticlimactic, so to speak."

"Shut up, Bobby."

"Shutting up now." His comment died in the air as she checked monitors and the sound level of the interior microphones. Bobby completed a similar equipment check, reached under the rearmost monitor, retrieved two headset/microphone rigs, and handed one to Terri. He plugged the headset into the jack on his end, while Terri did the same on hers. She adjusted her weapon, holstered in the small of her back, so she could sit comfortably. Bobby watched and shook his head as she turned to ask what was wrong this time.

"I still don't get why you won't do the shoulder holster thing. It works better."

"I've told you before. The damn gun is too big. Makes me look like Quasimodo. This works better for me. Not like I'm allowed to use it anyway."

"About that, Terri..." She stiffened as she became aware that it was time for "the talk." "I seem to remember that we were talking about your enigmatic behavior before work interrupted. We need to talk about this."

She grimaced. "Why? Why does everyone want to hear about my dark, scary thoughts?"

"You know damn well why. Because they're dark and scary and because you don't talk about it. It's been six months and you're still restricted." He held up a hand as she started to interject something. "Maybe you've been so busy trying to slay the dragons in your own head that you've forgotten that this affects me too. That makes it my business, whether you like it or not."

Terri stopped as the realization hit that Bobby was indeed correct. "Terri, I do get it. I really do. I've always respected that you like to keep some things, especially big things, to yourself. And I've never pushed before, but this isn't getting any better. This need you have, this—" He waved his hand indicating that the right phrase wasn't available. Terri filled in the blank.

"Patented Agent McKinnon stoicism."

He pointed right at her, indicating that the phrase was exactly what he was looking for. "Yes, patented Agent

McKinnon stoicism. That sounds like something Jen made up."

"Yeah, that's one of hers."

"Well, she's right. I guess that's why she's a college professor. But it doesn't take a rocket scientist to see that this is eating you up from the inside. I want to help. I know you're not sleeping right. I can see it all over your face. You're exhausted and it hurts to see you like this."

As she watched the monitors and listened for any sign of life in the dimly lit warehouse, Terri tried to collect her thoughts. "You know, Bobby, Jen and I had this same conversation two nights ago. She said exactly the same thing that you're saying now. Considering that I now have two corroborating testimonials that my own attempt to fix things is failing miserably, I should probably listen to both of you."

"Fuckin' A right you should." She turned to look, registering the edgy tone of his comment, as he waved it aside. "Sorry, that sounded harsher than I meant it. I just worry about you; that's all."

"I know you do. I'm really sorry about that."

"Terri, we're way past the time for sorry. Besides, I know you are. How about if you tell me what's going on."

Terri pushed the button to activate the proximity alarm for the camera. Allowing the electronics to take over, she sat back. She knew he was right, just like Jen had been. "Bobby, it's like this. You know that I've had trouble with nightmares. I did tell you that much. I relive the shooting over and over again, except it doesn't turn out the same way. I told the shrink this last week. My gun doesn't go off and I have to watch Jen get her brains blown out. It's really horrible, Bobby."

He blew out a long breath, evidently collecting himself to

respond. "Jesus, Terri. No wonder you can't sleep."

"No kidding. And there's also the issue of all the stuff that Davis told me about Jen. Do you remember that? When he called me?"

"I sure do. He said some nasty shit about her working you and some kind of illegal stuff that she was into. That wasn't true, was it?"

"Actually, some of it was true. I finally asked her about it."

"Which part?"

"The illegal hacking part. The details don't matter. She did something stupid a long time ago, and I just didn't want to know about it. Too honest for my own good, I guess."

"Are you okay with that?"

"I guess I am. Well, honestly, I wasn't when she told me, but I've figured out that she's right. It was a long time ago, and she knows better now." Terri sat forward, crossed her left ankle over her right knee and began to idly pick at the ever-present white cat hair around the hem of her blue jeans. "You know, it's like I found this really cool, happy thing, and I just wanted it to be perfect. And now I find out that it's not. I know that sounds ridiculous, but I came so close to losing her, and I royally screwed up along the way. You got hurt, I got shot, and it was entirely my fault. It was only dumb luck and the power of Kevlar that let me get to her in time. I just don't trust myself right now."

"Terri, I get that. I was worried at the time that you weren't thinking clearly, and I should have done something. Been more insistent that we needed help, but I wanted to believe you. I knew you were thinking with something other than your head, but I didn't call you on it, so that makes me just as responsible.

It wasn't all your fault."

"What did you think I was thinking with?"

"I was going to accuse you of thinking with your dick, like you always tell me, but I realized that you can't think with something that you keep stuffed in a sock in the top drawer of your nightstand." He let the crass nature of his comment sink in and watched Terri's mouth fell open in shock. "I knew that you were thinking with your heart and not your head, because I could see the way you just turned to Jell-O when she looked at you. I should have done more. This really isn't completely your fault, Terri. You have to believe that."

Terri noted that the pall of guilt that had become such a fixture in her mind suddenly felt a little lighter. Maybe he was right. She couldn't fix everything, especially considering that it wasn't all her fault. It wasn't all her fault.

"Terri, are you okay? What are you thinking?"

"First off, we don't keep it in a sock. Gets fuzz all over it. Secondly, I really might be okay. I guess the Bureau was so eager to make this all someone's fault that I believed them when they said it was mine. We all did things that we shouldn't have... you, me, McNally, Jen."

The quiet of the darkness was broken by the sound of an approaching vehicle that she recognized wasn't a car, but a motorcycle. Terri instinctively ducked, an action that was mirrored by Bobby, despite the windowless nature of their vehicle. She craned her neck to look out the windshield as the motorcycle stopped fifteen yards ahead of the van. The rider killed the engine and pulled off a helmet, shaking out long, dark brown hair in the process. As the rider stood up and climbed off the bike, it became apparent to Terri that the person under the leather riding gear was decidedly female. She heard a small whistle from behind her.

"Holy shit, Terri. I may be queer as a three-dollar bill, but I can appreciate a fine ass when I see one."

She waved him down, shooshing him at the same time. The thought crawled through her head that the leather-clad brick shithouse, who was now hanging her helmet on the side of the bike, was the reason they were here. Terri reached out to turn off the proximity alarm for the camera, quietly pushing the button as she watched every move of the dark figure. The stranger left the side of the bike and quickly disappeared from sight as she rounded the corner and headed for the entrance of the warehouse.

As soon as the woman was out of sight, Terri returned her attention to the video monitor, waiting patiently as she heard the door of the warehouse open and then close through the hidden microphones that fed into her headset. Bobby hit the button to start the video capture equipment, and Terri did the same with the digital audio recorder. Both agents leaned forward to watch their monitors. Nothing to do now except wait to see what happened next. Oh, and try not to stare at the brick shithouse's ass.

CHAPTER NINE

Denny bounded up the stairs to her apartment, juggling her backpack and a small bag of Chinese takeout as she tried to get her free hand to the carabiner clipped securely to the belt loop of her khaki pants. She unlocked the deadbolt for her apartment and pushed the door open with her foot. "Hi, honey, I'm home!" She snickered at her own joke since she lived alone and there was no one to answer.

She took time to check the mailbox, pulled out an assortment of junk mail, and tossed it onto the cable spool in the middle of the room. Since there was no mail of any interest, and no one to say hello to, she stopped long enough to consider calling her mother in Staunton to check in. She checked the date on her phone, noting that it was Thursday. Shit. Bingo night. Mom would be at the VFW with Aunt Betty, both of them chain smoking and laughing every time some lucky person shouted "Bingo!" and three-hundred people muttered "Shit!" Denny missed bingo night, the last thing she could really share with her mom, despite her disdain for the noise and the smoke. Their relationship had become strained since Denny had decided to come out to her; and was strained even further when she'd announced her intention to attend grad school away from home. The small city of Staunton was definitely not a hotbed of action for the average twenty-three-year-old, even less so for someone with Denny's interests. She had hugged Mom good-bye, encouraged her to visit when she could, promised to do the same, and headed for the big city.

Well, that was then. This is now, and right now, she had work to do. The mysterious project was coming along. She'd managed to get partway into the system, bypassing routers and firewalls along the way, but still couldn't get to her goal. Maybe tonight. She knew Faith would be calling in a short matter of hours, and she wanted to have good news for her. Denny pulled her laptop from her backpack. She swung open the lid of the computer, powered it up, and went to the kitchen for a fork and a can of Coke.

Briefly contemplating getting a plate, Denny looked around and decided against it. Mostly because she hadn't done the dishes for a few days, and none were available. Forks were in short supply too, but washing one was easier than wrestling with the provided chopsticks. When she returned to the living room, the computer was up and running, almost ready to go. She offered a brief hello to the downloaded photo of Keira Knightley (mmmm, pirates!) that took up the full screen of the computer, pulled out the containers of food, peeled them open and began to eat. In between bites, she opened her e-mail.

"Hmmm, spam, spam, penis size, ewww, spam, Oh, Dr. R. What you do you want?" She clicked on the message and began to read.

Denny,

Don't forget. Lesson plans on Monday. Also, I have another department meeting tomorrow (Friday). Can you cover debugging class at 2 p.m.? They're taking a test, so you just have to answer questions as necessary. Let me know.

Thanks

Dr. R.

Denny took a quick moment to shoot a response back agreeing to cover the class. No other mail of any interest, but that was hardly unusual. She debated checking her favorite message board to see what had happened during the day, but opted to just skip it, not wanting to get sucked into a discussion or a long round of movie/actor game. She had too much work to do.

The written notes that she'd started at the beginning of the project were getting longer every day, but she needed the benchmarks to remind her of the doors that she'd already opened to skirt around the advanced security measures in place in the system. There was some seriously advanced programming at work here, but Denny was confident that she'd get through. It was just a matter of time and motivation.

Time was always a problem. She had lots of responsibilities for school, including lesson plans and the preliminary work on her thesis project. Motivation. That part was easy. Denny was definitely happy with the extra cash as she wiggled her toes from within a brand-new pair of blue suede Vans. The new white American University baseball cap was nice too, not to mention the occasional stop on the way home for McDonald's or some other experiment with ethnic carryout. Definitely beats the shit out of a thirty-five cent package of ramen noodles, she thought.

And then there was Faith. Now there was a mystery. Definitely fell into the motivation category. Faith was an enigma, but she was an enigma that loved to flirt. Shamelessly. Aggressively. Flirt. And Denny had absolutely no inclination to discourage Faith's attention. Their second meeting had included drinks, as promised, as well as much more flirting.

She had met Faith in a nearby club, talked some about the project, had a drink or two, danced a little, and gone home. Denny enjoyed the memory, inwardly wondering if it could really be called dancing. Bumping and grinding were better words for the way Faith had danced with her. Their meeting... date...whatever it was ended abruptly as Faith announced she had to meet with someone else and left, stopping long enough to plant one truly wet, very open-mouthed kiss before heading out the door, leaving Denny a quivering mass of hormones.

"Shake it off, Robertson. Work, remember?"

Denny returned her attention to the monitor of the laptop. Using her notes, she retraced her earlier steps, but landed right back in the same spot that had halted her previous attempts to retrieve the desired files. She stopped, stared at the screen, and tried to think of a new way past the firewall that stood between her and the data. A new idea popped into her head. A few more keystrokes and the target files appeared.

"Cool! There you are. You're encrypted, but there you are."

Denny stopped for another forkful of spicy pork and a swig of Coke as she studied the encrypted file on the screen. To the average person, it would have looked like alphanumeric gibberish, but Denny saw something. Something she could use.

She typed in an advanced decryption algorithm and fought the urge to squeal with delight as the letters and numbers began to shuffle, reorganizing themselves into something that made sense. Her delight quickly faded as she made out several words in the file.

"Ebola...legionella...anthrax...bubonic plague...what the fuck!"

While Denny would be the first to admit that she wasn't exactly up on things in the news, she definitely knew these were not words normally associated with alternative fuel sources, as the paperwork for the project had told her. She'd have to ask Faith about it when she called. The wait proved to be short. As if on cue, her cell phone rang. She pulled it out of her pocket, checked the caller ID, and said hello to Faith.

"How's it coming, D?"

Denny hesitated, not quite sure how to answer the question. "Umm, it's coming. I found something and decrypted it, but it's still too protected to download. It's also weird...not sure it's what you want."

"Okay. Don't worry about it. I'll be over in a couple minutes to check it out. I'm sure it's what we want. Sit tight, D."

Before she could get an answer out, the call was terminated on the other end. Denny stared at the phone, shook her head, and snapped it closed. The phone found its way onto the top of the cable spool as Denny turned her attention back to the monitor. Again, the wait proved to be short as she heard heavy boots on the steps outside. Before she had a chance to get up from the edge of the futon, the door swung open and Faith stepped into the apartment.

"You should remember to lock your door, D." Faith

waggled her eyebrows. "Anyone could just stroll right in here." The look of mirth on her face morphed into an expression of something that Denny couldn't quite identify, as she added another thought. "Don't want anyone messing with you...well, besides me."

Denny watched Faith stroll over to the edge of the futon and flop down next to her on the cushion. Actually, right next to her. So close that Denny could feel the heat of one leather-clad leg, pressed tightly to the poly-cotton blend surrounding her own. She started to explain her concerns about the file, but Faith was quicker, offering up another comment.

"New shoes, huh, D? Very nice."

She looked down at the shoes in question."Yeah, my old ones were pretty shot."

Denny became aware of a hand making its way down the inside of her thigh, past her knee, and down to her ankle, pulling up slightly on the hem of her slacks to study the new shoes.

"Yes, very nice. I like them." The hand left her ankle.

Denny closed her eyes and took a deep breath in an attempt to collect her thoughts before she asked, "Umm, the file? Do you want to hear about it?"

"Sure." She leaned in and looked at the monitor as Denny pointed out the odd words in the file. Faith provided an explanation.

"Gotcha, D. I can see why this got your undies all bunched up. You see, this is about alternative fuel sources in Africa. That's the master document anyway. This nasty-sounding stuff has to be about the risks involved with working in Africa. I was pretty sure you'd find something like this. Don't worry about it."

Denny wasn't convinced. "Umm, okay. If you're sure..." Her words trailed off, replaced by nothing but shock as Faith turned and got up on her knees, straddling Denny's lap, pinning her to the futon.

"I'm sure. There's nothing to worry about."

Any thoughts of Ebola or risky work in third world countries flew out of her head as Denny saw nothing but tits. Inches from her face. Those tits. Holy shit. She became aware of a voice as Faith dropped her head to whisper.

"Go ahead. Touch 'em. I know you want to."

Denny swallowed. Hard. She tried words, but there were none. Her mouth became totally dry as all the moisture in her body traveled south. As much as she wanted to touch, Denny couldn't move. The voice whispered in her ear again, urging her to make a move. Any move.

"I've seen you looking. Go on. Do it."

Denny raised her shaking hands to do as commanded, as strong hands on her shoulders pushed her back harder into the futon, popping the ball cap from her head. Faith grabbed it, tossing it aside like a Frisbee as she leaned closer to Denny's face.

"I want you to."

As her hands finally found their targets, Denny took a ragged breath, gasping as her fingers closed around those luscious tits. Faith reacted, arching her back, as Denny squeezed the pliant flesh that was now pressing forward urgently, forcing itself into the palms of her hands.

"Good girl. I knew you could do it."

Denny gasped again, still unable to speak as Faith began to rock and grind into her lap. She heard a noise that she couldn't quite identify, but somehow Denny knew that the source of the sound was not Faith.

"You like that, do you?"

Denny grunted like a caveman as she devolved into a puddle of hormones and lust.

"That sounded like a yes. Was it?"

Still no language. Denny nodded from her slack-jawed haze.

"Thought so."

Faith moved quickly, shaking Denny partway out of her fog. She knelt in front of Denny and gave a quick yank to the frame of the futon. Denny fell backward with the futon as it converted from sofa to bed. She briefly processed that she was now looking at the ceiling, but there were no other thoughts in her head. Just those tits. And look! Now they were back. Denny registered the motion on the bed as Faith returned to straddle her, grinding her crotch into Denny's. Faith pulled on Denny's limp arms, encouraging her hands to return to those magnificent tits. Denny was gone. Checked out. Bye-bye.

Well, maybe not totally gone. Denny was able to process hands. Hands on her own less than ample breasts. Squeezing lightly, just enough to make her even less coherent, like that was even possible. Her breath caught in her throat as the hands moved away, slowly working one button open, then the next, and so on as her oxford cloth shirt fell open, revealing her plain white cotton bra. That stayed in place as the hands returned to her nipples, pinching them hard enough to feel wonderful, but not enough to hurt. Denny was about to check out for good, when she heard the voice back in her ear as the tits reappeared inches from her face once again.

"You've done this before, right?"

Denny nodded. Where was that damn English that she'd spent so many years studying in school? She had done this before. Not a lot, but enough to know what she was doing.

"Good...that's good to know."

The bed moved again. Denny became aware of that as Faith got up, pulled off the brand new sneakers, and removed khakis and boxers in one quick motion, not even bothering with the button or zipper of the loose-fitting pants. Denny was too far gone to even blush as her trousers and underwear hit the other end of the futon. But not so far gone that she failed to register the return of the hands. Hands working their way up the inside of her thighs. Thighs that fell mindlessly open, welcoming the hands, begging for more intimate contact. Fingers finally touching where they were needed most.

Denny heard Faith whistle. "Damn, D. I should have brought my snorkel and fins. I think we're gonna need a bigger boat."

Denny groaned, unable to do anything but press forward toward those eager fingers. She groaned louder as the fingers slid home. She didn't know how many. She didn't care. She just prayed that they wouldn't stop. They didn't. Neither did Denny, as she rocked up into the thrusting fingers, welcoming every stroke with a moan or a grunt and an arch of her back.

Just when she had decided that it couldn't get any better, it did. A warm mouth joined the party, wrapping soft, full lips around her clit as the fingers kept right on going. Denny screamed. Scared the hell out of herself in the process, but it definitely was a scream. More unfamiliar sounds spewed forth as a tongue joined in, driving her toward the edge as the movement of the fingers picked up speed and intensity.

Denny had no idea what to do with her own hands. They eventually found their way to the dark brown tresses attached to the head working furiously at the apex of her thighs. She twined her fingers into the hair, pulling the hot mouth tighter against her, dimly hoping that she wasn't doing anything painful to Faith, but not really caring either. She kept pulling as she felt heat in her lower back, followed by a chill down the back of both legs. Denny was coming, and she was coming hard. She began to wail as her climax became everything she was, just for a moment. See ya, Denny!

But then it was gone. The tongue was gone, the mouth was gone, and the fingers were gone, replaced by an emptiness that almost made Denny sad. Almost. She was sweaty now, her heart was racing, and she was breathing hard like she'd just come in from laps after softball practice. But this was so much better than that. Way lots better.

Denny pulled her hands away from all that hair, reaching out toward Faith. She got nothing but air in return as Faith was back on her knees, kissing Denny softly, placing one hand in the space between Denny's breasts. The voice was back.

"You okay, D?"

Denny decided to try talking again. She croaked out a broken sound that vaguely resembled the word "yes," cleared her throat and tried it again. "Yes, I'm okay. Wow."

Faith chuckled. Denny tried to pull her close once again, but Faith eluded the move. "Next time, kiddo. I need to split."

"What?" Denny sat up, lounging back on her elbows as Faith got up from the bed. "You're leaving?"

"Sorry, D. You just looked so tense. Thought I'd help. You

do feel better, right?"

Denny stared at Faith while she took a brief inventory of her own feelings. "Yeah, I do." She shook her head, attempting to clear her thoughts as Faith bent over, offering a warm, wet kiss.

"You're welcome. You're a great kid, but I really do have to go. Gotta check in with the boss. Besides, you have work to do, too."

Denny nodded, not yet trusting her voice or what she would even say. Work. Okay.

She watched with lingering disbelief as Faith grabbed a paper napkin from the Chinese food bag, wiped her hands and face, crumpled the napkin, and tossed it into the trash can next to the cable spool. Then Faith headed toward the door. Just before she pulled the door closed behind her, Faith turned, winked, and made a deal.

"Next time, D. Promise. Oh, and be sure to lock the door."

Denny never got a chance to answer as the door closed. Faith was gone. Again. And Denny was alone with her project. Again. Until next time. She could hardly wait.

CHAPTER TEN

Simon "Skip" Bradford sat quietly in his penthouse office suite. He had a problem. The Chief Executive Officer of Oakton Bradford Worldwide had a big problem. As he reached across the polished mahogany surface of his desk toward his Rolodex, one perfectly white cuff, with a gold Cartier cufflink attached, peeked out of the sleeve of his Hugo Boss suit. He needed help with his problem.

The guy from Information Systems, whatever his name was, had just left, but not before dumping the problem squarely on the immaculately restored eighteenth-century surface of Skip's desk. Usually, he wouldn't bother with something as insignificant as computer problems, but this was different. This was big. He would have to fix it himself, but he needed assistance from outside the company. That would require calling in a favor; an old favor left over from his college days. Skip flipped through his Rolodex with one hand while idly running the other through his hair, barely reorganizing the three hundred dollar haircut from earlier that afternoon.

Skip found the number he needed and removed the card

from the Rolodex. He reached for the phone on his desk to have his secretary place his call but stopped. That wouldn't work this time. This call needed to be private. He reached into the inside pocket of his hand-tailored wool suit and pulled out his BlackBerry. This conversation needed to be kept off the books, so to speak. Rolodex card in his left hand, phone in his right, Skip placed his own call.

As he waited for an answer, Skip sat back and swiveled his executive chair around, away from his desk, so he could look out the window over the cookie-cutter tech buildings and constant flow of traffic that marked the landscape of Northern Virginia. He hated the suburbs, but the operating costs in Washington proper had necessitated the move, and the sprawling office parks of the suburbs offered that touch of anonymity that Skip needed to carry out his work. His incredibly lucrative work that was now becoming problematic.

The phone rang twice before a male voice on the other end answered. Skip returned the tentative hello with a boisterous greeting of his own.

"Bulldog! It's Skip. How's life, my friend?"

Skip could have sworn he heard his old friend grin on the other end. "Skip...Skip Bradford. It's been a couple of years. How are you?"

"Ah, Bulldog, you know. Wildly successful, handsome as hell. The same. What about you?"

This time Skip heard the laughter. "Yeah, sounds the same to me. I'm good. Helen and the kids are good. Adam made the all-district team this year. Starting quarterback."

Skip rocked quietly in his chair, eager to get down to business, but fully cognizant of the need to play it right. "Good for him, Bulldog. You must be puffed up enough to pop."

"Well, Skip, you do know me. I'm forced to relive the glory days vicariously now. Time's an evil bitch that way."

Skip knew the feeling well. "Yes, my friend, that she is."

"But that's not why you called."

Bulldog always did have a way of cutting to the chase. "No, that's not why I called. I need your help, Bulldog. Have dinner with me tonight. We need to talk, and I don't want to do it here. And I definitely don't want to do it anywhere near your place."

There was that laughter again. "No, my place is definitely not a good choice. How about Artie's out in Fairfax? Nice place, great martinis—"

Skip interrupted, "Best steaks in the metro area according to the *Post*. Love it. Great idea. How about seven? I'll have my secretary call and get us a table. I'll even send a car for you."

"Seven sounds good. I'll call Helen and let her know. I think it's her bridge night anyway. And, thanks, but I don't think the car is a good idea. I'll drive myself and meet you there."

Skip remembered how pragmatic his old friend had always been. "You're right as always, Bulldog. We can finish this at seven. I'll see you there."

Artie's at seven. Always a good plan. He hit the button, ending the call, and slipped his BlackBerry back into the interior confines of his suit. He reached across the expanse of mahogany and pressed the button for the intercom.

"Elizabeth?"

He began to idly play with his hair again while the secretary answered. "Yes, Mr. Bradford?"

"I need you to call Artie's over in Fairfax and reserve a table for two at seven. Then please call my driver and have him pick me up at four thirty. I have racquetball at five."

"Artie's at seven, racquetball at five. Anything else, Mr. Bradford?"

Elizabeth was always so efficient. He appreciated that. Maybe she needed a raise. Well, maybe something simple like an early afternoon off would make her happy. "No, Elizabeth. That's all I need for now. Why don't you make those calls and take the rest of the afternoon off? I can take care of myself for a couple of hours."

"Yes, Mr. Bradford. Thank you."

Skip sat forward and pressed the button to end the call on the intercom. After a quick debate with himself regarding the appropriateness of single malt scotch mixed with racquetball, he opted to forego the drink. He still had a problem to think about.

Time passed quickly as it often did for Skip. There was never enough time. He made some phone calls, checked his stocks, put out a corporate fire or two. The usual stuff. He worked diligently, finally stopping to check the time. "How did it get to be four twenty already?" he asked softly into the air to no one. Time to get moving. He got up, shuffling papers in the process and reached for his briefcase. A small stack of paperwork found its way into the depths of his ridiculously expensive Italian leather bag. Skip snapped it closed and headed for the elevator, down to his waiting car, making a quick mental note to speak to the building manager about the lousy choice of elevator music. Maybe some soft jazz would be better. Definitely better than the Montovani arrangement of "Girl from Ipanema." Just how clichéd was that? Skip deserved better.

He approached the black Lincoln Continental, gave the

driver a curt greeting, and climbed into the back seat. He had confidence in his driver, enough to know that his gear for the gym was stowed securely in the trunk. The ride was short, barely allowing enough time to reconsider his problem. The car stopped gently at the front door of the Crystal City Gateway Sport and Health Club in Arlington. Skip thanked the driver, exchanged his briefcase for his gym bag, and strode into the club.

Racquetball, like everything else in Skip's life, was played with people who knew exactly who was in charge. Laughing as the club pro intentionally missed an easy return, Skip never let on as the, "Great shot, Mr. Bradford," reached his ears. The game went on like this for close to an hour before Skip tired of the continuous stream of ass-kissing from the pro and excused himself to prepare for dinner with Bulldog. One quick shower followed by a change into his freshly-laundered shirt (thanks to the club), back into his expensive wool suit, and Skip was on his way out, off to meet Bulldog. Off to fix his problem.

The Lincoln pulled up just outside the front door of the restaurant. "Please wait for me. I'll call you when we're done." Skip opened his own door and stepped out into the early evening. He was early, but only by about ten minutes. He chose to go inside and order a drink. Artie's did, after all, have the best martinis in the metro area. Skip fought the urge to channel Sean Connery as he ordered a Stoli martini with three olives. He really didn't give a good goddamn if it was shaken, not stirred, so long as it was vodka and not some kind of cologne-flavored gin, and was served painfully chilled.

The bartender slid the drink across the bar, and Skip was not disappointed after his test sip. It was indeed the best martini in town. He gave his approval to the bartender, turned his attention back to the front door, checked his Rolex, and began to wait for Bulldog.

Right on time, the front door opened and his old college buddy stepped into the restaurant. Skip smiled, as he looked Bulldog over. Nothing had changed; from the dark gray suit and college striped tie, to the steel gray brush cut and the demeanor of a pit bull with a migraine.

Bulldog, known to the rest of the world as FBI Supervisor George McNally, met Skip's glance, acknowledging his presence with a quick nod. Skip hailed the bartender and pointed to his drink, silently requesting a second one for McNally, and then turned back, offering a combination handshake/hug to his old pal. McNally spoke first.

"Looking pretty good there, Skip."

Skip pulled himself up to his full six feet, two inches, patting himself on his still flat belly in the process. "Ah, you know, Bulldog. Takes a lot more work than it used to."

McNally patted his own not-so-flat belly in response. "Don't I know it? Living vicariously through my kids hardly keeps me in shape, but I just don't have the time."

Skip clapped McNally on the shoulder. "Who'd have ever thought? Bulldog McNally, starting fullback for the Penn State Nittany Lions, big man at the FBI, reliving the glory days through his kids. I just never saw you going down that road."

McNally offered a wistful smile and a shake of his head. "Neither did I, Skip. Neither did I. But you—"

"Me?" Skip interrupted with raised eyebrows, indicating his interest in McNally's next comment.

"Yes, you. Starting tight end, corporate mogul, and

permanent fixture on *Metro Magazine's* list of Most Eligible Bachelors. Settling down just isn't in the cards for you, is it, Skip?"

Skip waved the question aside. "Nah, not for me. Too much work to do. C'mon, Bulldog. This eligible bachelor needs a big fat steak."

"Sure," said McNally.

Skip grabbed both drinks off the bar, handed one to McNally, and led the way to the hostess station. After being escorted to a private table in the back corner, Skip sat facing the entrance and offered McNally the less desirable position of back to the door. When the waiter arrived, Skip ordered two T-bone steaks, medium rare and a bottle of Bordeaux.

McNally tested his own martini, and jumped right in. "You said you had a problem. How can I help you?"

Skip took another swig of vodka laced with vermouth. "Ever the pragmatist, eh, Bulldog? I do have a problem. I think our Kazakhstani friend is back and nosing around in my business. Can't have that, Bulldog."

McNally answered with a look on his face that Skip couldn't quite decipher. "Yeah, I thought so. I've heard a thing or two. Actually sent two agents out last week to check up on that trained bitch that works for him. You remember, the one with the motorcycle?"

"Oh yes, I most definitely remember her. Faith whatever-her-last-name-is-this-week, right?"

McNally nodded and took another sip of his martini. "That's her. I wasn't sure why she was back in town, but I have a much better idea now. You want me to pick her up?"

"No. I need to know who she's working with. I've got a

hacker problem with some new research we've been doing, and I need to plug the leak. Can you put your people back on it to follow her? Find out who she's wrangled into working for her this time?"

"That won't be a problem. I'll get a couple of feelers out to see if we can establish any patterns. Might take a day or two. Once I have that, I can put two teams of agents on it full-time." McNally took another drink and sat back as the waiter arrived with salads. "I've got a head case agent that I need to keep busy. She hates this kind of thing, but she's chomping at the bit to get out of the office, so I know she'll do it without a fuss."

Skip furrowed his brow. "Head case? Is that a good idea? And what about her partner? Won't that be a problem?"

"Nah, she's a good agent. Very organized and totally by-the-book. She's only a head case 'cause she killed a perp six months ago and got the willies about it. I have some reason to suspect that she was, and still is for that matter, screwing the perp's target. That would go a long way toward explaining her problem. I can use the fact that said target happens to be female also. Agent McKinnon won't give us any problems."

"And her partner?"

"Same thing...no problem. He'll do anything for her, and that includes chasing all over hell's half acre, following a crazy bitch on a motorcycle. Plus, I have just as much reason to suspect that he has a weak spot for the college-aged boys in Dupont Circle, and I can use that if I need to. We're all good here, Skip."

Skip smiled and pushed his empty salad plate to the side. "I hope so, Bulldog. Are you sure you're still working for the FBI, or have you taken a job with the Village People?"

McNally made a similar move, pushing his salad plate to the side, making room for the steak now being presented by the waiter. "Easy there, Skip. There may be some confusion between the two of them about who's supposed to be screwing whom, but they're top-notch agents. I don't really care who they fuck as long as the job gets done."

"That's very open-minded, Bulldog. Good for you. I suppose next you're going to tell me that you vote Democratic and drive a hybrid vehicle."

McNally glared. "I wouldn't go that far." Both men laughed companionably as they dug into their steaks. "Definitely not that far."

Skip ate in silence, savoring the perfectly prepared T-bone. Pulling Bulldog out of a rock quarry thirty-five years ago, unconscious and half-drowned was still the smartest thing he'd ever done in his life. Having an FBI supervisor with a debt to pay in your back pocket was a good thing. Skip raised his glass of wine to McNally, who returned the gesture warmly.

It was a very good thing indeed.

CHAPTER ELEVEN

Terri sat in the office biting her nails and waiting for the therapist. She was far too nervous to even attempt the magazine thing. She was so tired of this place with its softly colored walls, ergonomically correct furniture, and soothing lighting. It was as if everyone who walked through the door was somehow dangerous and in need of calming. Terri glanced at the receptionist and noted a look on the woman's face. Annoyance, perhaps, with a tinge of sympathy. It didn't take long to figure out the receptionist's problem, as Terri ran the laundry list of her own jittery behaviors. Biting her nails, shifting in her seat, crossing and recrossing one leg then the other, and wiggling her foot like a little kid in need of a potty break. She planted both feet firmly on the floor and took a deep breath to collect herself.

Terri, slow down. It's going to work this time. You've talked to everyone. You know what you need to know about Jen, and it was a long time ago. You talked to Bobby; even told him about—Oh, shit! You told him about the stuff in the nightstand. That was stupid. Oh, well, it's done now. And you didn't tell him about all of it. That's good. Easy, Terri. You need to play this cool. Maybe...

Terri almost leapt from her chair, offering a quiet "Sorry" to the startled receptionist, as she crossed the small waiting area to look out the window. The fifth floor offered a spectacular view across Pennsylvania Avenue. Much better than the view out her own second-story window that faced the opposite direction, offering only an obstructed view of the buildings housing the Department of Agriculture and the Department of Energy. She realized suddenly that she'd lived in the DC area for close to ten years and had never been to visit the Jefferson Memorial. That had to be rectified.

Tomorrow, Terri. Do it tomorrow. It's Saturday, the weather is supposed to be nice, the leaves are changing. Pack up a picnic, grab Jen, and go. You need the break, she needs the break. Why not? Or, hey, screw the picnic and just go. Was that the phone? Go somewhere nice for lunch, walk around the Memorial, make out behind a tree—

"Agent McKinnon?"

Terri turned, pulling her attention out from behind the tree in her head, and redirected it toward the receptionist. "Yes?"

"She's ready to see you now."

Terri answered with a soft "thank you" and made a beeline for the office door, her hand coming to rest on the doorknob long enough to steel herself for the therapist.

You can do this, Terri. You can have everything back, and all it's going to cost is the right answers. This time...

She pushed the door open, maybe a little too hard, and stepped into the office.

***

Fifty-two minutes later, Agent McKinnon was back. She fought the urge to run, screaming for joy, into the hallway and back toward the office. Instead, she stopped long enough to thank the receptionist and dig her phone out of her pocket. Calling Jen had been the original plan, but she decided that the surprise would be better, and Jen was in class all afternoon anyway. She called Bobby instead, who answered on the first ring.

"Terri, how'd it go?"

"Well, if you're still driving out to the range today, I need a ride. I have to requalify." Terri yanked the phone away from her ear at Bobby's whoop of joy. Terri could see the scene in her head as she imagined Bobby ducking in embarrassment at his own noisy response.

"Aw, shit, Terri. That's so cool! I knew you'd kick this thing's ass."

Terri was thrilled beyond all reason, but she let Bobby keep going. She knew him well enough to be certain that she wouldn't be able to get a word in edgewise anyway.

"C'mon, kiddo. Hurry back. I'll buy us lunch to celebrate on the way out to the range."

"Five minutes. I am still in the building after all." It didn't take long before she was in the stairwell at the opposite end of the hallway, running back down toward the office. Terri was barely through the door leading back to the second floor before she found Bobby, who promptly swept her up in one of his patented bear hugs, easily removing both of her feet from the floor. While she admired and welcomed his enthusiasm, Terri needed him to stop.

"Bobby... air...."

He quickly set her down, but kept his hands on her shoulders, holding her attention. "See, I told you so. Now, tell me all about it. What did she say? What did you say?"

"I'll tell you everything. I promise, but not here. Let's go change and get out of here. I have a pressing need to be outside and away from this concrete monstrosity today."

"Good idea, Agent McKinnon." He offered a conspiratorial wink. "Besides, McNally's out for the day. We don't have to come back." Bobby turned and started toward the elevator, but Terri stopped him by grabbing a sleeve of his jacket.

"Stairs are quicker."

Twenty minutes later, Terri was out of her suit and into cargo pants and a sweatshirt, Bobby in similar attire. She waited patiently in the parking garage, watching and grinning while Bobby took the convertible top down on his Firebird. He opened the passenger side door of the car, urging her in, as he ran around the back of the car, slamming the trunk on the way. Terri laughed, noting inwardly that it was her first real laugh for months, as Bobby vaulted over his own door and landed hard in his seat. She slid on her sunglasses as he did the same, pointed toward the exit of the garage, and said, "That way. Let's go blow stuff up." Bobby gunned the engine, and peeled out.

After a short stop for sandwiches and drinks, Bobby's treat as promised, Terri sat at the firing range, lounging on the hood of the car, sandwich eaten, leaning against the windshield in the autumn sunshine. Bobby was noisily finishing his lunch, attempting to get the details of Terri's visit to the therapist.

"So what did you finally tell her to get reinstated?"

Terri stretched the last kink out of her back and returned to her best snake-on-a-rock pose. "I just told her what she wanted to hear. I'll be a good agent, I'll think everything through, and even if you or Jen has a gun up your nose, I'll stop to call for backup." She turned and noted the puzzled look on his face. "What?"

"Is that really what you said?"

"Yep, that's what she wanted to hear, so that's what I told her."

"So, in other words, you lied to her?"

"I prefer to think of it as a creative interpretation of the truth in order to get what I wanted."

"And you're just okay with that?"

Terri could only huff lightly and try to defend her choice. "Bobby, what choice did I have? I told her the nightmares were gone too."

"Are they gone? The nightmares, that is."

She shrugged. "Pretty much. I hope. It's been almost a week since the last one. I've talked to you and Jen about it since then. Maybe that did the trick."

Bobby grabbed a napkin out of the brown paper bag that had once contained their lunch. "Terri, I want to believe you, but I'm not sure that was the right thing to do. I mean, I've seen some things out of you in the last six months that I never thought I'd ever see from you, and now you're lying to the therapist—"

"Bobby, I need—"

She stopped as he held up a hand to interrupt. "Terri, I know what you need, as well as what you thought you had to do to get it, but I'm still worried that this wasn't the right decision."

Terri fought against her own exasperation to answer his concerns as he defiantly crossed his arms over his chest. "But what was I supposed to do? This has gone on long enough and the only way I can prove to anyone, including myself, that I'm fit for duty is to get back to work and show everyone that I'm okay. You certainly get that, don't you?"

"Yeah, I do. I'm just worried about you, that's all. You get that, right?"

"Yeah, I do get that, and I appreciate that you worry about me, but it's kind of tough to slay the dragons if they lock you out of the castle and take away your sword."

"Maybe you're right. I sure hope that you're right. Getting back to work will probably do more for you than all the therapy appointments you've had to sit through in the last six months."

"Bobby, I can promise you that this will all work out." Terri approached him and reached out to offer him a reassuring squeeze to the forearm. "Besides, if it doesn't, you can be the first in line to kick me in the ass. Okay?"

Terri released his arm to walk over and retrieve her weapon from the car. She started to walk to the range, sliding her gun into the holster at the small of her back, which forced Bobby to run in order to catch up. After a quick stop with the agent in charge to sign in and check out ammunition, Terri headed straight for the stationary target zone. Bobby joined her at a table while she loaded three clips for her weapon, sliding one into her P-228 with an audible click, and thumbed the hammer release. Bobby did the same while she put on her protective earmuffs and stepped forward to shoot.

Since target practice conversation was basically impossible, Terri shot her required sixty rounds, scoring an impressive ninety-two percent, well above the eighty percent required to qualify. Bobby, mature as usual, stuck his tongue out as he showed her his ninety-four percent score. Laughing, she waved him off. "I haven't been out here for six months. Next time, pal."

"Want to check out a shotgun? You could use the practice."

"Sure. Jen's got class until four. Let's do it." As she returned to the agent in charge to log her qualification, Terri mused, thinking how good it felt to be back. The weapon felt good, felt right in her hands. She was back in control, just the way she liked it.

Shotgun practice went much the same, conversation limited by circumstance. Bobby stopped her with a light tap to the shoulder. "Go ahead, do the thing. I know you want to."

Terri shifted the shotgun to her left hand and chambered her last round with a smooth, one-handed maneuver. Bobby threw his head back, howling, and said, "God, if Jen could just see you now. That little move would get you so laid."

Terri answered with a knowing smirk. "You think?"

Terri fired off her last round and checked her watch. She pulled off her earmuffs. "Speaking of which, how about we get out of here? I think I want to be home soon."

He answered with a knowing smirk of his own. "Anything you want, Agent McKinnon."

***

The ride back into town from Quantico was companionable, but could never have been described as silent. Terri sat back with her eyes closed, basking in the sun and wind as Bobby cranked the radio and sang along, loudly. She enjoyed his slightly off-key rendition of some old dance song that she didn't remember, silently wishing that something would come on for her to sing along with as well. That would have been nice.

As they hit the downtown section of DC, Bobby turned down the volume on the radio, which pulled Terri from her reverie. "Terri, are you asleep? You're awfully quiet."

"Just enjoying the day. It feels good to have that monkey off my back," Terri answered quietly, as she let her hand drift out the window to hang glide in the draft.

"I bet you are." Bobby directed his attention fully on the road. "I'd ask if you wanted to go out later, but I'd imagine you have plans."

"What kind of plans do you think I have?"

Bobby nearly spit, "Oh, please, girl. You are officially reinstated, you've been to the range, and you reek of gunpowder. Do you honestly think that Jen is going to let you out of the house tonight?"

Terri started to come back with a smart-assed quip, but stopped as full realization hit. "Well...umm...no."

"There you go." Bobby rounded the corner, pulling up in front of Terri's townhouse. "And here you go. Home at last."

Terri pulled the door open while Bobby shut off the car, and removed the keys to open the trunk for her. Jen's 4Runner was already parked in the driveway, a fact that caused Terri to blush, provoking another barrage of comments from Bobby.

"Jeez, Terri. You only need to see the car and you start to change colors. Give it up, kid. I know you too well. I'll call you tomorrow."

She ducked her head into the trunk, grabbed her bag and suit, and wished her face didn't always betray her. Acceptance was the only option, so she hiked her computer bag onto her shoulder, accepted one last congratulatory hug from Bobby, slung her suit over her arm, and said good-bye. She watched as Bobby hopped back into the car, started it up, and pulled away in another squeal of tires.

CHAPTER TWELVE

Jen squeezed her eyes closed, steeling herself against the images crawling through her brain. How could she let something like this happen? Her anxiety level began to climb as she realized the full depth of her problem.

Rosenberg, remember to breathe.

She did just that, inhaling deeply through her flared nostrils as she struggled against the barrage of sensations coursing through her addled brain. Any attempts to move or struggle were futile. The cold steel of the handcuffs biting into her wrists served as ample reminder of her plight. If that wasn't enough evidence for the brilliant college professor, the strong hand in the middle of her back, holding her down, served nicely as People's Exhibit Number Two. Jen tried in vain to look behind her to see what was going on, but that only served to raise the ire of the officer in charge, whose soft voice provided a sharp contrast to the strength being used to maintain control.

"Dr. Rosenberg, if you'd just hold still and cooperate..."

She didn't. Jen's continued attempts to free herself only made it worse as the hand on her back applied just enough pressure to make it clear that escape was not going to be possible. She finally relaxed a little, more out of a sense of resignation than any desire to "hold still and cooperate." She heard the soft voice in her ear once again.

"There you go. That's better. This doesn't have to be difficult now, does it?"

Jen shook her head, choosing to remain silent rather than to allow her voice to betray exactly how nervous she was. It really didn't need to be difficult. It was just a release of control, a demonstration of trust, but one that she was having a little trouble with. She took another deep breath to calm herself as the thought passed through her head that this was exactly the position she'd imagined herself in. Actually, she'd seen herself in this position before, plenty of times, just never outside her own head. Her thoughts drifted back as she took stock of the events that led to her current predicament.

"Are you sure, sweetie?"

"Yes, Terri, I want you to do this. I really do."

Looking for something in Terri's soft blue eyes, Jen saw exactly what she was searching for. Support, more than a little arousal, and most importantly, unconditional love and trust. She could do this. Hell, she wanted this as badly as she'd ever wanted anything in her life. Steeling her resolve, Jen smiled at Terri, who offered her one last chance to back out.

"Because, if you're not sure, I don't—"

"No, baby, I'm completely sure. Just a little nervous. You know?"

Terri smiled, once again reminding Jen exactly why she was so smitten and eager to try something like this.

"Sweetie, I'd be a little worried if you weren't nervous. I

know we kid around about this a lot, but it's a big step. It takes a lot of trust."

Jen turned from her seat on the edge of the bed and took both of Terri's hands in her own. "I trust you."

"I know, but this is a lot. Do you think you need a safe word?"

Jen was puzzled. "Safe word? That seems a little extreme. But if you think that...I mean, I didn't know, you know? Well, maybe you don't, but I thought...I don't know what I thought. It's just, I hadn't...well, not that I hadn't, but kind of just..."

"Jen, breathe."

"Right. Breathing now." She hadn't thought that far into it before, but, as usual, Terri was right. "Mainframe."

Terri chewed lightly on her lower lip. "Mainframe. That makes sense."

Jen watched Terri's face again, making special note of her eyes and the way her pupils dilated. Jen could see that Terri obviously wanted this too. She leaned in, offering a soft kiss and a hug.

"Yes, mainframe. So what happens next? Do we—"

She never got the rest of the question out because Terri was already moving. Jen had never before seen her in full cop mode, and was startled by the speed and power that she demonstrated. Further contemplation of the situation flew out the window as Terri jumped up from the edge of the bed, pulled Jen up by the shoulders, flipped her over, and shoved her face first back onto the bed. Jen, too surprised to react as her face hit the comforter, soon became aware of a strong hand in the middle of her back and a commanding voice in her ear.

"Hands straight out, palms up." Jen hesitated, a little

unsure, but not for long as Terri made her demands clear. "Now!" She moved to comply.

Jen felt a twinge in her shoulder as her right hand was pulled into the small of her back. She couldn't see what was happening from her facedown position on the bed, but the gentle pressure of a knee on her left arm kept her sufficiently immobilized while the jingle of a pair of handcuffs provoked a rush of adrenaline, quickening her heart rate and breathing. Jen felt a second rush, considerably south of her chest, as the cuff snapped into place around her wrist and the knee was removed from her other hand, which was soon guided into place, joining its partner at the small of her back. The second cuff closed around her wrist, and Jen came to the full realization that nothing short of safe-wording was getting her out of this.

Not that she really wanted out. It was just a little overwhelming.

Terri evidently sensed this as Jen's thoughts snapped back to the present. "You okay, sweetie? Do you want me to...?"

"No. Please..."

Jen had no idea what was coming next. Her inability to see Terri's face was proving to be more than a little disconcerting, but the soft voice was back, close enough that Jen felt warm breath on her ear.

"Good girl. I thought so." The hand left the middle of her back, and Jen shuddered as it drifted lower, caressing gently downward until it came to rest on her backside. Closing her eyes, Jen attempted to rein in her anxiety as the soft touch of the hand on her butt was joined again by the voice in her ear. "You're in a little trouble here, Dr. Rosenberg." Jen swore she could feel the amusement that sounded from deep in Terri's chest. "Definitely a little bit of trouble. Now what are you going to do about it?"

Jen again attempted to struggle against the restraints, but gave up quickly as she felt the cold steel holding her hands in place.

Yeah, like she said. Definitely a little bit of trouble.

"I don't think that's going to help you here. Maybe I should try to come up with something." Jen became aware of motion again as Terri's hand drifted down her right leg, back up her left, all the while teasing around her inner thighs. She groaned when the hand finally worked its way back up, stopping at the crotch of her pajama pants. Jen felt the color rise on her face as she and Terri came to the mutual realization of exactly what effect the scenario was having on Jen.

"Jesus, Jen. I'd always suspected you'd like the cuffs, but I'm quite frankly awed by how warm things are getting down here." Jen fought to breathe a little as she squeezed her thighs together, attempting to keep Terri's hand snugged up against her. It didn't work. Terri pulled her hand away and offered a small warning.

"Dr. Rosenberg, do we need to have a little chat about the chain of command here?"

Jen only shook her head to indicate that she was fully aware of the rules of this new game, closing her eyes against what was starting to become panic, a look that she knew Terri would be unable to see.

"Good. Glad to hear it. But we still have a small problem." Jen craned her neck around again to try to see Terri's face, but the angle made that impossible. "What am I going to do with you now? Seems to me like I could pretty much do anything I want, doesn't it?"

In an attempt to ascertain the true depth of Terri's commitment to their game, Jen didn't answer right away, but changed her mind quickly as the hand returned to the middle of her back and Terri's almost whispered words sounded in Jen's ear.

"I asked you a question."

Jen's response amounted to only the slightest inclination of her head, indicating that Terri could do anything she liked, and the thought provided an additional wash of anxiety for her. From their first time, Jen had almost always initiated their sexual encounters. She was the flirt, the maker of suggestions. Once things got rolling, she usually backed off and let Terri take the lead, but she still felt in control. This was different. She really needed to step back and let things unfold; it just wasn't easy for her.

Just let go, Rosenberg. It isn't that hard.

Well, it shouldn't be, so why was it?

You want this, Rosenberg. You've wanted this for as long as you can remember. Right? She'll let you go if you say the word, but you're not gonna say the word. It's a fantasy, doofus...what you've always wanted. Do it for her. She's your cop, your fantasy come true. You've had dreams about this; hell, you've almost wrecked the car thinking about this. They're just handcuffs and Terri has the key. It's right there on the nightstand. That's all it is. What you wanted. The keys are on the nightstand, aren't they? Isn't that where she put 'em? I hope. Fantasy. C'mon Rosenberg. This is for her. This is what you want. Breathe, Rosenberg. Do it for Terri. No, really, Rosenberg, breathe. In and out. You can do this. Do what you need to do. It's simple.

Just do it. Just take a deep breath, and—

"Mainframe."

She almost couldn't hear herself actually say the word, but there it was. Jen fought not to panic because it seemed to appear that Terri almost didn't hear it as well.

"What? Jen...Sweetie, are you okay?"

Jen began to struggle again, fighting and pulling against the handcuffs as Terri reached over to the nightstand to get her keys. "Yes, baby, but please. Mainframe. Let me go. I can't do it."

"Easy, sweetie." Terri offered a soothing touch to the center of Jen's back as she returned with the keys. "I'm here..." She unlocked the cuffs, much to Jen's relief. Jen lay flat on the bed and tried to push the anxiety down, an action that was so very much easier with the handcuffs tossed aside, out of reach. She rolled over onto her back, attempting to rub away the sensation of the manacles, still very much aware of her discomfort and the way those damn cuffs felt. She relaxed a little more and closed her eyes to enjoy the touch of a soft hand to her cheek as Terri checked in.

"Jen, are you okay?"

"Yeah, baby, I'm okay." She sat up, and searched Terri's face, finding exactly what she needed. "I'm so sorry. I really wanted..."

Terri offered a quiet "shh" and pulled Jen close for a comforting hug. "It's all right. I don't want you to do anything that makes you uncomfortable."

Jen pulled back, extricating herself from the hug to try to process her jumbled thoughts.

"Baby, I know, but I really thought... I mean, shit, I don't know what I thought. I've thought about this for like, well, forever. Well, maybe not forever, but you know what I mean." Terri listened, allowing Jen the opportunity to vocalize her concerns and work through her problem out loud. "We've talked about this, we've joked about this, and now here we go, and I lock up. What's that all about?"

Terri shrugged. Jen hoped for an answer. She could tell that Terri was thinking, trying to come up with something supportive to offer, and waited as patiently as a hyper-intelligent college professor who had just safe-worded her way out of a pair of FBI handcuffs could wait. In other words, not very patiently.

Terri eased her from her discomfort gently, offering both words and a soft touch to Jen's knee. "Jen, first off, you know that I'm not disappointed, right?"

"But, Terri, you wanted to do this—"

Jen was silenced again with a gentle touch to her lips. "Sweetie, I wanted to do this for you. Think about it this way. I leave this house every day with those handcuffs tucked away on my belt. Just like my gun, just like the pen in my pocket and my phone. It's stuff for work. When I have to use the cuffs, it's not for fun; it's to restrain a criminal, and to protect myself. They're not toys to me. Actually, they're not really anything to me. Just stuff I take to work."

"I mean, it's like your briefcase. You take it to work every day. It's not like USB drives and floppy disks make you hot, right?"

"Actually..."

Terri could only huff with mock disgust. "What was I thinking? My mistake. But you get my point. I do this cop thing for work. It's a huge turn on for you, and I want to give you what you want. The fantasy is fun and hot, but the reality is that handcuffs are confining and evidently a little more than you're comfortable with."

Jen remembered exactly how confining and uncomfortable those handcuffs felt. Since it seemed to be time for processing feelings, she shifted enough to sit cross-legged on the bed, and took Terri by the hands. Terri pulled her feet into the same position and faced Jen , as she attempted to put her additional concerns into words.

"You know, the part I don't get is why I reacted the way I did."

"You mean the claustrophobia?"

"No, baby, I mean the fact that I'm still sitting here in wet underpants." Jen offered a lopsided grin as she tried to piece together the odd mix of sensations. "As totally uncomfortable as it was to freak out like that, parts further south are trying to tell me that I liked it. So what's that about?"

Terri shrugged. "You still like the fantasy, right?" Jen nodded vigorously in response. "Maybe it's just that." Jen grinned knowingly as she watched the expression on Terri's face change from concern to flirtation. "Or maybe since you have your hot cop right here, you couldn't stand the thought of not touching me. I'm pretty partial to that theory."

Jen took Terri's hands and pulled her close, whispering, teasing in that special way that she knew that Terri always responded to. "Or maybe you smell like gunpowder and you used your hot G-man mojo to addle my brain into submission."

Terri laughed, an easy sound that made Jen feel like everything was all right again. "Yeah, that's it. I did that so I could get your hands out of the cuffs and over your head..."

Jen followed Terri's instructions and found herself in a compromising, if not restrained, position, "...lay all over you and say really naughty things in your ear."

Discussions of discomfort appeared to be over, so Jen finally let go of the last of her anxiety. "I like that plan. So, Agent McKinnon, what kind of naughty things were you thinking of?" She watched Terri's eyes shift to the right, toward the top drawer of the nightstand, and understood exactly what she had in mind.

"Again, I say good plan, Agent McKinnon. Why don't you strap that bad boy on and see what kind of trouble we can get into?"

Terri rolled over onto her back, and sat up on the side of the bed. Jen watched Terri intently as she pulled the drawer open and started removing items, arranging them on the bed with her usual sense of organization. Jen shuddered as the green silicone dildo hit the comforter, feeling her nipples harden in response. She could see that Terri was studying her reaction. Jen's suspicions were confirmed as Terri said, "So, Dr. Rosenberg, I can tell that you see something you like."

"Well, you are an FBI Agent, after all. How did you deduce that?"

"Actually, it hardly takes a detective to see that. If your nipples were any harder, they'd poke holes in your shirt."

As she raised her hands to cover her own breasts, Jen cursed softly, "Dammit. Busted by my own traitorous nipples, huh?"

"Yeah, that's pretty much it." Terri pushed Jen gently back into the comforter, applying slight pressure with a hand in the center of her chest. "But you mentioned something else. Something about wet underpants. Is that still a problem?"

Jen scooched her butt around on the bed, attempting to ascertain the actual condition of her underpants. "That's an affirmative, Agent McKinnon."

Jen shuddered a little as Terri opted to let her fingers do the walking, sliding them slowly up the outside of Jen's legs, up to the waistband of her pajama pants. Jen shuddered again as strong hands grabbed at the elastic, pulling both jammies and underpants off in one smooth motion.

There were times, lots of times actually, when Jen could tease and play around like this for hours. This was not one of those times. "You know, Agent McKinnon, I think you might need to do a little more investigation here."

"Oh, do you now?" Terri's hands were back, this time creeping slowly up the insides of Jen's thighs, applying a gentle pressure to move her legs just a little wider. "What do you suppose...oh my God, Jen." Terri stopped as her fingers located the cause of the wet underpants. "You really weren't kidding."

"Nope, I wasn't. And I think since you are to blame for this condition, that you should take immediate action to fix it."

So she did. Terri flopped onto her belly, arranging herself strategically to bury her face into all that wet, stopping long enough to nibble her way up the inside of Jen's thighs, adding just that little element of torture to Jen's already heightened arousal. Jen groaned, offering a small warning, "Terri..."

"What? Need something, sweetie?"

"Please, baby...don't tease... I need you."

Please don't make me beg. I need you. I can feel your hot breath on my pussy, and it's driving me crazy. Just a little to the right...little more...yeah, right there.

Jen moaned as Terri hit the spot with one long swipe of her

tongue. "Is that better?"

"Oh God, baby. Yeah...better." She rolled up with her hips in order to keep the lovely, talented tongue as close as possible, and fought the urge to rock harder.

Easy, Rosenberg. Don't break her nose. That would be a good one to explain over at the ER. Well, you see, Doc, she was licking me...going down on me just like that...oh shit... yeah like that, and it was really good... oh God it was so good... just like that...Hey!

"Terri, what... where'dja go?"

Through her haze of want, Jen watched Terri get up on her knees and rock back onto her heels, answering, "I'm still here, but I need a couple of minutes to take care of something that you mentioned earlier." A look crossed Terri's face, one that Jen knew intimately, as a potentially wicked idea struck Terri. She reached up and gently guided Jen's right hand to her own pussy. "Take care of this for me for a second...I'll be right back."

Jen groaned at the sight of the completely naughty expression on Terri's face as she watched, for just a moment, as Jen took care of herself.

Yeah, I see you looking at me. Oh, baby, you have such a dirty mind, and I'm the only one who knows it. Here, check this out...

Jen applied enough pressure with her splayed fingers to open herself up fully, offering Terri a totally unobstructed view. Terri's breath hitched once...*gotcha!*...just enough to let Jen know that her actions had landed for the desired effect, as she held herself open with one hand and used the fingers of the other hand to explore, easily sliding just the tip of one finger into herself.

Look at you, Ms. Big Bad Agent. You'd better close your mouth before you start to drool and take a breath before your head explodes. Hell, I'd better slow down or I just might explode. Easy there, Rosenberg. Don't break the nice detective.

"Terri...baby? You still with me? I thought you had something to take care of."

"What? Yeah... oh, sorry... right. Hang on."

Wits apparently regained, Terri began her preparations, sliding the green silicone dildo into its appropriate place and rolling a condom down its length. She got up to remove her cargo pants and underwear, replacing them with a black leather harness. Satisfied that the straps were adequately tightened, she climbed back onto the bed, removed Jen's hand from its assigned task, sucked the juice off her fingers on the way, and pulled Jen up onto her knees. Leaning in as Terri kissed her, hard, Jen thought she just might lose it right then and there as Terri ended the kiss, pulled back and said, "I want you on top. I want to watch you."

I bet you do. Well, let's just see what it's worth to you.

Jen pushed Terri back onto the comforter roughly enough to surprise her. Terri's eyes widened, and Jen asked, "How bad do you want that?"

"What?"

"You heard me, Agent McKinnon. How bad do you want to watch me... watch me fuck you?"

Ooh...that got her. You felt that everywhere, didn't you?

"Oh, God...Jen...please..."

Hands on Terri's shoulders, Jen pinned her to the mattress and leaned in, offering soft words and a nibble to her ear. "Please, what, Agent McKinnon?"

You're not getting off that easy, Missy...say the words.

"Please, Jen..." Terri hesitated as Jen's hands found her breasts, not-so-gently teasing out her nipples through the ribbed knit of her black tank top. "Climb up on me, slide down my cock, and fuck me."

Yeah, that's it. Good girl.

Jen registered the gentle pressure of hands on either side of her waist, urging her up and onto a little over seven inches of textured bright green silicone. She pushed down, taking most of it at once, eyes rolling back as she adjusted to the fullness.

Ooh, that's nice. Little speed bumps of joy.

The pressure around her waist aided Jen once again, helping her to push down, urging her to take more. It got easier each time as Terri helped Jen find a rhythm, encouraging her, teasing out a moan as she released Jen's waist to slide up under her borrowed scarlet and gray football jersey to fondle the small breasts within.

Good shot, Agent McKinnon.

Jen moved, up and down, as Terri rocked in counterpoint. She thrust up with her hips as Jen pushed down, increasing the tempo just a little each time. Leaning forward, Jen took Terri by the wrists, pinning them over her head, supporting herself while she rocked. Jen watched as Terri allowed her head to fall back into the pillow. "Hey...I thought you wanted to watch."

Terri's eyes snapped open. "Oh, yeah... that's right."

"Maybe this'll help," Jen teased, sitting back a little as she released Terri's left hand, pulling her right one up to suck on her first two fingers. "Help me out here." She pushed Terri's hand down, closer to that hot, wet place that was quickly becoming the only thing that Jen could think about. "Touch me, baby.

Help me come."

Terri groaned. So did Jen, as wet fingers found her clit, circled it, made it swell in response.

"Better, sweetie?"

Like you had to ask.

"Oh, yeah. That's what I needed. Oh, God...Terri, please... do that some more."

Jen kept thrusting, while Terri kept rubbing, pinching, and squeezing. Groaning out a question, Jen asked, "Do you like that?"

"Mm-hmm..."

"Do you want me to come, baby?"

"Oh, yeah... do it."

Five... four... three... two... one...blastoff!

Jen came, like a freight train, as she growled her release and arched her back. She thrust down one last time, taking all of it as she grabbed Terri's wrist to stop the direct pressure. The hands returned to her waist, holding her securely as Terri thrust up with her hips, keeping Jen's orgasm alive like the last few flashes of lightning at the end of a thunderstorm.

Oh...wow.

Jen rolled off, landing hard on her back in a slightly sweaty heap. After pushing her wet bangs out of her eyes, she turned to look at Terri, making special note of the almost smug look on her face.

She knows she's so good at that. Mmmm...

"I love you, you know that, right?"

"Yeah, Jen, I know that. I love you, too."

"Especially when I come like that?"

"Especially when you come like that."

God, she's so beautiful.

Jen rolled over and propped herself on her elbow. "I want to make you come like that."

"Well, then...since I got reinstated today, I think that you should..." Terri hesitated as she threw her head back and opened her arms wide. "...have your way with me."

"Dealer's choice, eh?"

"Dealer's choice, Dr. Rosenberg."

God, I love it when she calls me that.

"Well then, give me this..." Jen got up on her knees and tugged at the black leather straps of the harness as Terri rolled off the condom, tossing it somewhere in the general direction of the waste basket. Jen got ready quickly, making sure that everything was just right as she pulled the straps tight, rolled on a fresh condom, and crawled her way back onto the bed. Jen pushed Terri's knees apart gently and walked up the inside of both thighs with her fingers. It didn't take long for Jen to ascertain the effects of what she had just done. "Jesus, baby... you're so wet."

"It's your fault... you do that to me...I can't..." Terri stopped talking as Jen explored, sliding through Terri's slick pussy with her fingers, stopping long enough to tease, just a little.

"Should I not do that? Do you want me to stop?"

"Oh... no, no..." Jen knew that Terri was having trouble. She could hear it in her voice, noting the special way it got deeper when Terri was aroused. She could see it in Terri's eyes, the way her pupils dilated and clouded over.

Be nice, Rosenberg. She wants it. She's ready. Well, maybe just a little more...

"Are you sure?" Jen dragged two fingers up, making sure

that Terri was truly ready. She was. Jen slid those same two fingers in, Terri's hips rising to meet her, as she leaned over Terri and supported herself with one arm. Jen let a naughty smile play across her face and reclaimed her fingers to offer Terri a taste of her own juice. Terri groaned from deep in her chest, a sound that spurred Jen on to tease a little more, painting Terri's lips with her own wetness. She watched as Terri licked her own lips, mesmerized to the extent that she didn't even see Terri's hand, as she reached up, tangling her fingers in Jen's hair to pull her closer.

Rosenberg...wake up. Kiss her, you dope.

Jen covered Terri's mouth with her own, dueling with Terri's tongue, tasting the delicious wetness that always made her lightheaded with arousal. Opening and closing her mouth gently against Terri's, Jen groaned.

Eloquent, Rosenberg.

Jen felt as her hair was released, the hand moving down over her shoulder. A second hand joined, trailing a similar path down Jen's other shoulder. The hands moved slowly, down and back up. The kiss never wavered even as the hands trailed lower. Fighting the urge to thrust, Jen willed herself to relax and enjoy the strong hands kneading at the pliant flesh of her backside.

Oh, that's nice. Mmmm... okay... hey, wait...what?

Jen yelped as her back hit the comforter, no time to react as Terri straddled her tummy and pulled their conjoined hands up over Jen's head. She leaned in to whisper, "So, Jen... do you want to see something really hot?"

Jen struggled to answer as a tongue buried itself most of the way into her ear. "Um...sure."

"Thought so," Terri answered. Somewhere in her addled

brain, Jen managed to process that Terri's voice was even lower than before.

Buckle up, Rosenberg. This should be good.

Terri sat up, pulled slowly on the bottom edge of her black tank top, lifting it up and off, sending hair flying in every direction, pulling about half of her ponytail loose in the process. Jen helped, sitting up just a little, as Terri tugged on the finished edge of Jen's jersey, pulling it off before tossing both shirts off to the side.

"Give me your hands, Jen."

Jen did, giving in as Terri pulled her hands up, encouraging Jen to touch her breasts.

Don't have to ask me twice to do that.

She squeezed and fondled, dragging her fingers inward to tease out Terri's nipples. Terri arched her back, leaning into Jen's touch.

"That's nice, Jen."

"Yeah, it is. That is hot, baby"

Terri leaned forward, close enough that Jen could feel hot breath in her ear again. "Oh, you ain't seen nothin' yet."

Oh my God.

Jen registered the tongue in her ear once again, and smiled as teeth gently closed around her earlobe.

"Watch this."

Jen complied, watching as Terri scooted down, reaching between her own legs to guide the dildo where she needed it to be. Jen thought she might just lose it as Terri slid down slowly, taking all of it, chewing on her lower lip. Terri's eyes closed as she rocked forward and pushed down again. Jen heard the deep groan that followed.

"Is that good, baby?"

Well, no duh, Rosenberg. Remember about ten minutes ago...

Terri rocked forward again, groaning what Jen assumed to be her assent. Jen placed hands on Terri's hips, moving with her, helping her to find a rhythm. Terri kept moving...just like that, baby...as Jen hung on and joined in with her hips. Just like Terri had done before, Jen thrust up as Terri pushed down, over and over again, until Terri stilled, pushing down hard enough to keep Jen from moving.

Huh?

"What...Terri...do you need something else?"

Terri leaned forward once again, offering Jen the hope of more naughty words and a tongue in her ear. She gasped as Terri stopped just long enough to bite her on the neck. Rolling her head to the side to offer better access to those lovely teeth, Jen whimpered with disappointment when it didn't happen again. She changed her tone quickly as Terri's tongue found her ear and then Terri was back to tease, just a little more.

"Yes, Jen, I do need something else."

Wow, she's like a baritone now. Woof.

"I need you to fuck me. I need you to put me on my back, slide your beautiful bright green cock into me, and fuck me 'til I scream." The tongue was back. Jen shuddered. "Can you do that, sweetie? Can you fuck me like that?"

Hell yeah, I can do that.

Terri pulled herself off, taking Jen by the hands to help her onto her knees. Jen asked, "Ready, baby?"

"Oh yeah."

Jen leaned over, hands on either side of Terri's head. She

reached down to guide the dildo in slowly. She felt Terri's hips rise to meet her. Jen braced herself on both hands then pulled back and thrust forward again. Terri's hands found their way to her ass as Jen alternated between a quick thrust and a slow withdrawal. Terri's hips rose, helping Jen to move as deeply as possible. Terri's legs replaced her hands and Jen felt ankles lock around her behind, pulling her in, holding her, letting her go, showing her the rhythm that Terri needed. Jen found it quickly and watched as Terri's hands fell to either side, balling up the comforter with her fists in perfect time to Jen's thrusts.

She could see the muscles in Terri's jaw clench and release as she rolled her head against the pillow and tried to speak. "Oh fuck...Jen..."

Oh fuck is right. Look at you, Agent McKinnon. You're sweaty, there's hair everywhere, and you're the most beautiful thing I've ever seen.

"Is that good?" Jen asked. "Do you need to touch yourself?"

"No," Terri shook her head and answered breathlessly. "Just do that. Keep doing that." She released the covers to grab Jen by the shoulders, raking short nails down her back, digging in almost painfully.

Mark me, baby. I'm all yours.

Jen knew all the signs. Months of experience had shown her the way Terri's neck muscles flexed, the way her jaw locked, the way her legs fell open even more. Terri was close and Jen knew it. She shook the sweaty bangs away from her eyes, pushing just that much harder and faster, giving Terri exactly what she needed in order to come. When she did, it was with a shout as she arched her shoulders up off the bed, holding Jen close, squeezing her tightly in synch with each wave of her orgasm.

Jen watched closely as Terri let her go and fell back against the comforter.

I was wrong. That's the most beautiful thing I've ever seen.
"Jesus, Jen."

Jen pulled out and rolled over, giving her knees a break, and asked, "You okay, baby?" She loosened the straps of the harness and slid everything off, tossing it toward the end of the bed. Jen rolled over to look at Terri then watched, puzzled, as Terri curled up into a ball and began to laugh. "Hey, what's so funny?"

Terri kept laughing, struggling to speak as the laughter trailed away into giggles. "I just can't believe some of the smutty things that come out of my mouth."

"Hey, I love the smutty things that come out of your mouth," Jen said. "It's nice that you know what you want, and if you have to be all jazzed up and naked to talk like that, well then, it's a sacrifice that I'm willing to make."

"Oh, are you now? You're always so willing to do the hard work, aren't you, Dr. Rosenberg?"

"Only for you, Agent McKinnon."
Only for you.

CHAPTER THIRTEEN

Denny stared at the monitor as she waited for the file to download. After days of creative attempts to skirt around the roadblock of firewalls, she had finally gotten into the server. The information was just as scary as the first time she had seen it, but since Faith had provided assurances that it was okay, Denny chose to trust her...her what? What exactly was Faith? Friend? Employer? Fuck buddy?

"Screw it, Robertson. Just download the file." Denny waved aside her own concerns and returned to the task at hand. It wasn't like they were dating. It really wasn't like they were anything, but Denny just couldn't clear her mind of the way she felt the last time Faith had come to visit.

"Next time, D. Promise."

Faith had promised a next time, and the words haunted Denny. "What does that mean?" She asked the question into the air, certainly not expecting an answer, but needing to ask it anyway. Frustrated and more than a little confused, Denny returned her attention to the monitor and waited not-so-patiently for the file to download, knowing full well that the "next time" that Faith had referred to could only happen if and when the information was safely decrypted and saved onto the USB drive that Faith had provided.

Denny wiggled her knee impatiently as the numbers on the download progress indicator continued to climb. Ninety-five percent. She reached for her phone to check the time as the number hit ninety-seven percent. Denny slipped the phone into her pocket as the numbers on the computer reached one hundred percent and the progress indicator told her that the files were downloaded. After taking a quick moment to save the files to the USB drive, Denny powered off her computer, packed it up, and headed for school. As much as she wanted to call Faith and tell her that she had the files, Denny had class in twenty minutes and she was running late as it was. She'd have to call her on the way and hook up later.

***

Terri's patience was in short supply. She fumed and shifted in her seat, finally forcing Bobby to act, or at least say something.

"Terri, will you please sit still? You're making me nervous, and there's nothing going on." Lowering his binoculars, Bobby asked, "Are you sure the tracer is working?"

Terri checked the receiver in her hand and noted the steady flash and accompanying beep of the tracer that she had hidden under the seat of the suspect's motorcycle. "Yes, Bobby, it's working just fine." She set the receiver down. Nothing happening there. She checked the monitor for the camera trained on the warehouse entrance. Nothing happening there. She turned up the volume on the headset, hoping for a snippet of conversation.

Nothing. Terri pulled the headset off and huffed. She crossed her left ankle over her right knee and then reversed them. If she had to spend one more second staring out the window of the surveillance van at nothing she was going to scream. "But this sucks, Bobby. There's nothing going on. And why the hell are we following this person anyway? Especially in the middle of the day."

"Ah, patience, Agent McKinnon." He watched out the same front window that she did, but he had the benefit of binoculars. "There's movement inside the building. Just keep an eye on that motorcycle, please."

Terri started to complain about something else, but stopped as the door to the building swung open, revealing the woman with the dark hair and fabulous ass that they'd seen on their first trip to the warehouse, sometime around a week ago. Terri started to say something, but Bobby beat her to it.

"And again I have to say, nice ass. Leather pants are always a good choice, especially with motorcycle boots. And given the way the weather is changing, the matching leather jacket—"

"Bobby, hush." She waved him down as she watched the suspect head for the motorcycle. "Just get ready to drive in case the transmitter decides to cut out on the first bump."

Bobby pulled on his seat belt and got ready to start the van. Terri looked back and forth several times between the motorcycle and the receiver in her hand, silently hoping that the tracer would stay put and that the ride to wherever they were headed wouldn't turn into a high-speed pursuit because of faulty electronics. She watched as the woman pulled on her helmet and climbed onto the bike, twisting the key to start the engine. A quick step on the shift pedal engaged the transmission, while the driver released the clutch to pull away from the warehouse. Bobby waited until the bike disappeared around the corner, pulling away only when he got the high sign from Terri.

Terri rode in silence while Bobby drove. She wondered why they were following this person, but more so, why their orders were to "Watch, follow, but do not apprehend." It just didn't sit right with Agent McKinnon, but she trusted McNally, and there must have been something going on that she and Bobby just weren't privy to. She shrugged and thought, "whatever," while she watched the blip of the motorcycle on her receiver.

She finally broke the silence with a question. "Can you still see her?"

"Yes, ma'am. Hot biker babe straight ahead. Is the tracer still transmitting?"

"Yes, sir, it is."

"And why do you think we're following her?"

"Bobby, I can't answer that, 'cause I just don't know."

They drifted back into companionable silence as Bobby drove through the sparse traffic, leaving Southeast and heading north toward a better part of town, and Terri watched the receiver in her hand to make sure that they were still going the right direction. Fortunately, the tracer was working perfectly, so Bobby didn't have to follow too closely, a fact for which Terri was abundantly grateful. The woman on the motorcycle seemed to prefer major roads, sticking to I-295 until she got the chance to get off the freeway, eventually making her way northwest on Connecticut Avenue. Terri smiled when Bobby waved as they passed Dupont Circle. She was pretty sure he was thinking what she was—wishing that they could stop by her house and take a break from the van. The traffic lights seemed to be in agreement with the babe on the motorcycle, so Bobby drove around the circle and onto Massachusetts Avenue toward American University, prompting him to ask another question.

"So Jen has class this afternoon?"

Terri watched out the window as they passed the buildings of the Naval Observatory. "Yep, last class is debugging at two o'clock, then she usually checks in with her grad assistant and heads out. Then she gets home at about four and works until I get there between five and five thirty."

"And then the fun begins."

She opted for the sarcastic response. "Yes, Bobby, then every day, as soon as I get home, I tie her to the bed and we have scorching hot lesbian sex until we're both too exhausted to move. I've actually thought about leaving the Bureau to become a dominatrix—oh, shit. Bobby, turn left at the next street."

He slowed the van, waiting for the oncoming traffic to clear in order to make his turn. "It's okay, I can still see her." He snickered.

"What?"

"You said dominatrix. There's a picture."

"Shut up, Bobby." She looked around the neighborhood, getting her bearings and noting the abundance of townhouses that had been turned into apartments for AU student housing. "Why do you suppose this person is cruising campus?"

Bobby shrugged while he scanned the neighborhood. "I don't have a clue, Terri, but I don't like it. If the Bureau is involved, then motorcycle woman is into something bad. I don't like seeing her around all these kids—wait. It looks like she pulled over up ahead." He frantically looked around for a place to stop. "Shit, there's nowhere to park."

Terri pointed out the window to a vacant driveway on the right. "Over there, Bobby, driveway. Just pull in and pretend we're the plumber—oh wait, she's off the bike and walking. Just pull it over. I'll take the sidewalk and you can hang back and follow me."

"Terri, wait—"

Bobby never finished the sentence. Terri was out of the van, pointing to the sleeve of her black leather jacket to indicate that Bobby should turn on his wire. Her earpiece crackled to life, and he checked in.

"You with me, Terri?"

She gave him a thumbs up sign, opting to remain quiet as she followed their suspect, hanging back about half a block, trying to be as inconspicuous as possible without scaring the hell out of the residents of the neighborhood. Terri stopped at the next corner and slid in close to the bricks of the house, peeking around the building to determine the destination of her target. She watched the woman trot up the steps leading to a converted house and let herself in. Terri slipped back around the corner to stay out of sight while she checked in.

"Bobby, suspect entered a house about halfway down the block. There's a driveway across the street. Pull in and park there. You should be able to see out the back of the truck. Let me know if I can get closer without being spotted."

"Roger that, Terri."

She peeked around the corner of the building one last time as Bobby turned left down the street past her and pulled right into the driveway that Terri had spotted earlier. She knew that the advanced electronics in the van included a rear-facing surveillance camera that would allow Bobby to check out the building with a minimum of crawling around inside the van. She gave him a minute to look around before she called back in.

"Bobby, talk to me."

"Okay, you can move again. Head down the street. Suspect is on the first floor. I can see her through the window, and she's obviously looking for something. There's a lower entrance to the building. You can hop the fence and hang under the steps until she's done. Hurry, go now."

Terri did just that. She scooted quickly down the street until she reached the house, hopped the knee high wrought iron fence that protected the lower entrance of the building, landing hard in a crouch on the concrete below, and waited while Bobby continued to watch the activity inside.

"Bobby," Terri whispered into her sleeve microphone, trying to remain as quiet as possible, while she stood to move further under the steps.

"Go ahead."

"Check the address on the computer. See if you can find out who owns the building."

"Doing that now. A rental company owns the building. I'm going to call them and see if we can find out who lives in the apartment."

Terri waved, letting him know that she understood. She slid in under the steps as she heard the door to the apartment open above her, followed by the sound of boots on concrete, stopping halfway down in their descent. Terri ducked a little further into the cramped space, cringing at the noise her leather jacket made as she moved, hoping that the ambient noise of the neighborhood would provide cover for the sound. It seemed to work as Terri heard a Zippo lighter and noted the empty red

Marlboro pack as its crumpled remains sailed past her to land on the concrete below the steps. She almost jumped out of her skin as her earpiece crackled to life with Bobby's whispered warning, "Hold tight, Terri. Suspect just sat down to make a phone call."

Since she had absolutely no choice but to do exactly that, Terri held tight and listened while the biker babe made her call.

"Hey, boss.... No, it wasn't here. She called me on her way to class, and I think she's there for a while, but I was hoping she'd left something behind."

Terri shifted to hear better, wishing that she could make out the other end of the call.

"Whoa, easy there. I know what I'm doing. I just wasn't planning on her going to class with everything."

Terri could hear the agitation in the biker's voice as she shot comments back to the person on the other end.

"Listen, dude. You're paying me a lot of money and I'll take care of your problem, but you need to back off and give me a little room to work here. I'll get the goods, and you can pack up your shit and head back to Whatthefuckistan before the end of the week. Chill, okay?"

Terri silently mouthed "whatthefuckistan" to herself, wondering what it meant. "Okay, Kazakhstan, whatever. I really don't care. What I do care about is getting you off my back so I can do what you pay me to do. We're all good here, so there's no need to get your panties in a knot. I'll call you later."

Terri heard the phone snap closed as the biker babe muttered a single word, "asshole," just loud enough for Terri to hear, before she was back on her feet and heading down to the sidewalk. Terri ducked back under the steps one last time, watching as a burning cigarette butt flew past her, following the same trail as the empty Marlboro pack from a few minutes earlier. She peeked out around the steps and waved to Bobby, who answered, "Okay, the whole thing is on tape and I've got a name for you. Don't answer me 'cause Ms. Slutbomb isn't clear yet. The rental company gave me the names on the lease for the three apartments in the building, so I ran them through the database while our suspect was on the phone. I think you may be interested in one of them. The studio apartment on the first floor is rented to an AU grad student, one Denise Robertson, formerly of Staunton and Harrisonburg. I don't believe in coincidence, Terri."

Terri almost choked on the name, clapping her hand over her mouth as she fought not to blurt it back to Bobby. She waited until he told her she was clear and then responded.

"Holy shit, Bobby. Did you say Denise Robertson? Is there a photo with the record?" Terri struggled not to dash across the street and shake the information out of him. She shifted nervously from foot to foot while she waited for him to answer.

"Yeah, Terri, there is. Ms. Tightpants is around the corner if you want to high tail it over here and see it. You should get moving anyway if we need to take off again to follow."

Bobby didn't have the comment all the way out of his mouth before Terri was moving, hurrying across the street to sort the mess out. It didn't help though as she jumped up on the driver's side running board of the van, reaching through the open window, across Bobby to get a better look at the picture on the onboard computer monitor, immediately recognizing the driver's license photo on the screen.

"Oh, shit, Bobby. This is not good."

"What? I told you I didn't believe in coincidence. How is she related to Jen besides the same hometown?"

Terri fought past her own panic to try to piece together an answer for him. "Bobby, Denise Robertson, otherwise known to her friends as Denny, is Jen's graduate assistant." Bobby mouthed a silent "oh, shit" as Terri continued, "Jen told me a while ago that someone approached Denny about some kind of cryptic job thing. She was concerned that it was one of those college hacking-for-cash deals, so she tried to talk Denny out of it. Well, evidently, Denny didn't listen, and now there's some babe on a motorcycle, working for some Kazakhstani bad guy, tossing her apartment looking for something." Terri stopped as she registered the sound of a motorcycle starting up around the corner.

"Oh, shit, Bobby. We need to stay with her, but I have to contact Jen and keep Denny from going home. Shit!"

Bobby tried to calm her down. "Terri, get in the truck. We'll follow her and you can call Jen and tell her—"

"No, you follow her. I'm going up to campus to talk to both of them. It's only six blocks north of here. I can walk it in ten minutes."

Bobby reached out of the window of the van, grabbing Terri by the front of her jacket. "No, Terri, you can't do that. McNally will have your head. You know we have to do this by the book."

"Bobby, stop. Let me go," she shot back through clenched teeth as she twisted out of his grip. "You stay with Ms. Slutbomb; follow her. You don't need to check in with the office until we get relieved at six o'clock. It's just now two. Don't say anything to anybody until then. Just stay on the suspect. I'll talk to Jen and Denny. Jen's in class until three. I'll text her and have her call me back and make sure she keeps Denny in the office until I can sort this mess out. I'll call you by four, and we'll figure out the rest of it then."

Bobby set his jaw and responded, pointing a finger at her face for emphasis. "Agent McKinnon, as your partner and best friend, it's my duty to tell you when you're acting unprofessionally. And believe me, sister, unprofessional doesn't begin to describe the crazy shit you're talkin' about now."

"Bobby, please," Terri pleaded. "We don't know what's up or why we're following the babe on the bike. We're totally in the dark and McNally seems to be okay with that. Well, I'm not. And now there's a possibility that someone close to Jen and, for all I know, maybe even Jen herself, is in on some bizarre shit that I can't even begin to understand. We've got mysterious babes on motorcycles tossing computer hacker's apartments, making cryptic phone calls to guys from Kazakhstan, and believe me, none of that adds up to someone wanting to buy Tupperware and ship it to Asia to store their Camel Chow." Terri fought back the tears that she felt coming on as her panic began to bubble through to the surface. "There's something big going on here, and someone I love more than anything might be involved. I can't sit in this fucking truck and wait. So unless you have a better idea, I'll call you at four o'clock."

Bobby hesitated, apparently unsure what his next move should be. The sound of a motorcycle passing their location snapped him into action.

"All right, Agent McKinnon, but if this goes south..."

"It won't, Bobby. It's just a side trip to find out what's really going on. Please trust me."

Bobby nodded, but the set of his jaw told Terri she was skating on thin ice. He threw the transmission into reverse and pulled out of the driveway. Terri began to walk north toward campus, hesitating as her earpiece crackled to life with the sound of Bobby's voice. "Please be careful, Terri."

She answered, talking into her sleeve. "I will. Thank you, Bobby." And just like that, he was gone, roaring off in the opposite direction to chase after the mystery woman on the motorcycle. Terri pulled her cell phone out of her pocket, flipping it open to send a text message to Jen, walking and typing at the same time.

"Call me ASAP. Minor 911."

Terri quickened her pace, striding purposefully toward campus, and hopefully some answers. Her first problem was solved quickly when her phone rang. She flipped it open and answered, listening as Jen launched into a barrage of questions.

"Baby, what's wrong? Are you hurt? What's going on?"

She slipped into the closest approximation of her soft agent demeanor as she could manage. "Jen, I'm okay. Do you know where Denny is?"

"Denny? Yeah, she's in debugging class with me. I left her in charge so I could call you. What's going on?"

"I'll explain it all when I get there. I'm on my way to your office right now. Whatever you do, don't let Denny leave before I can talk to her."

"Terri, what the hell are you talking about?"

She stopped walking long enough to collect herself to answer. "Jen, please, just do this for me. I'll explain it all when I get there. I'm only about ten minutes away. Go back to class and make sure that Denny comes to your office as soon as it's over. Maybe you can get her to stay with the class right now and I can explain everything in your office before she gets there. Please, sweetie, trust me on this."

Terri heard Jen's frustrated huff of breath on the other end. "Okay, Agent McKinnon, whatever you say. I'll get Denny to take care of class and I'll meet you outside."

"Thank you. I'll be there in a few minutes." Terri started to close the phone, but stopped, offering up one last thing. "I love you, you know that?"

"Yeah, baby, I do. See you soon."

Terri kept walking, resisting the urge to run. She crossed the street, and passed the sign that welcomed her onto the main campus of American University. Once on campus, she took a moment to collect her thoughts. Part of her knew that Bobby was right. She should have stayed in the van, but the bigger part of her, the part that couldn't deal with the fact that Jen might be in danger again or worse, somehow involved in this whatever it is, won out. Maybe she shouldn't be back on the street again, but that didn't matter anymore. It was too late to worry about it now. For now, she had one objective: get to the bottom of this mess with Jen and Denny and sort out her career later.

CHAPTER FOURTEEN

Terri kept her head down and her sunglasses on as she marched purposefully across campus toward Jen's office. Her black leather jacket was quickly proving to be too warm for the early fall day, but she opted to leave it on rather than to advertise to the student body at large that she was an FBI agent, and one that was armed and wired for sound at that. She could feel the sweat start to break out between her shoulder blades, but ignored it as best she could, focusing on her goal. Passing Bender Library as she crossed the Quad, Terri spotted Jen on the front steps of McKinley Hall, pacing nervously with her cell phone in her hand.

As happy as she was to finally spot the understandably agitated Jen, Terri couldn't help but be a little nervous, still unsure of what she was going to say beyond the obvious, "Hey, sweetie, did you know that your grad assistant is hacking databases for a Kazakhstani mystery man and his motorcycle riding babe of a henchman? Oh, and by the way, I just had a major panic attack meltdown of some kind and are you working for him too?" Despite what she'd said to Bobby earlier, she knew that Jen would be as clueless as she was, but still felt more than a little bit of concern that mistrust was the first place her thoughts had gone.

Steeling her resolve against her own discomfort, Terri spoke quietly to herself, "Again, Agent McKinnon, it really is kind of late for that now." She watched Jen's expression change when she spotted Terri. The worry and agitation drained away. Terri wished she could say the same. She purposely left her sunglasses on, a line of defense that she used frequently to hide behind when she was unsure of her feelings and how to present them. Jen reached for Terri and gave her a comforting hug.

"Hey, you." Jen pulled back, but didn't let go, in an apparent attempt to ascertain Terri's problem and the level of her concerns. "What's going on here?"

Terri took a deep breath to try to center herself. She resisted Jen's attempt to pull her up the steps by the hand and into the building. "Can we just stay out here for a minute? It's quiet and we can talk."

"And you don't have to take your sunglasses off, right? This must be really bad." She grabbed Terri by the hand, this time not accepting no for an answer. "Upstairs, Agent McKinnon. You yanked me out of class for a so-called 'minor emergency,' so I'm entitled to some answers."

Terri reluctantly gave in and allowed herself to be pulled into the building and up to Jen's second floor office, passing the computer lab full of debugging students along the way. Jen ushered Terri into the office, closed the door behind her, and offered her a chair next to the desk. After removing her sunglasses and storing them safely away in the inside pocket of her jacket, Terri welcomed the opportunity to shrug out of her black leather, hanging it on the back of the chair as she adjusted the weapon holstered in the small of her back in order to sit more comfortably.

"Again, Agent McKinnon, what is going on? And why did you need to talk to Denny?"

Terri hesitated, trying to pull all the disparate pieces together in her own head. "It's a long story, so I'll just cover the high points. Okay, you know that Bobby and I have been out on surveillance duty, right?"

"Well, I did figure that out, yes. I know you can't talk about the who and why kind of details, but I know you've been following some bad guy around for a few days."

"Right. That's it. Anyway, the person we've been following decided to take a ride into town and make a little stop at the apartment of an AU grad student named Denise Robertson."

The look of utter shock on Jen's face confirmed Terri's belief that Jen knew nothing about Denny's activities, whatever they might be. "Wait, it gets better. I got out of the truck and followed our subject down the sidewalk. The details aren't important, but I managed to get close enough to listen to this mystery person while she made a phone call to her boss."

"She? You didn't tell me—"

"Yes, she. Sorry I left that part out. Unfortunately, I don't think this was just a social call from Denny's biker babe friend. While I was outside, listening under the stoop, the suspect tossed Denny's apartment looking for something. She did that before she made her phone call. She sat out on the stoop, called her boss, and made some comments about not finding what she was looking for. She figured Denny must have taken whatever she was looking for to school with her. Then she said that she'd get 'the goods...'" Terri punctuated the last two words with air quotes, "and that he could pack up and head back to Kazakhstan by the end of the week. I remembered that you told me something about Denny and a strange job offer, so I put two and two together and wound up here."

Jen just stared, dumbfounded. Terri had never known her to be at a loss for words. "Does this make the slightest bit of sense to you, sweetie?"

"Well, I'm not sure. I mean, I can only assume that Denny took the job, and now she's gotten herself way in over her head. Terri, this is just weird, and I'm honestly not sure what to think. Kazakhstan? Really? I did tell her to stop by here when class was over. I didn't tell her why, but we usually do that anyway, so that part doesn't worry me."

"So what are you worried about, well, despite the obvious?"

"Actually, I'm mostly concerned that I have no idea where Bobby is. You were working together today, right?

"So, now it's my turn to put two and two together. You heard the conversation from the babe on the bike, Bobby did the computer thing and figured out that it was Denny's apartment, and it would seem that you freaked a little and took off without him. Am I close?"

"Well, yeah, pretty close."

Terri swore she could see the light bulb snap on over Jen's head. "And the first thing that crossed your mind was one of two things." She held up a hand, counting off her first point with an extended index finger, "One, that I was in some kind of trouble, or..." she raised another finger, "two, that I'm involved somehow. Please feel free to jump right in anytime and tell me that I'm wrong."

"No, Jen, you're not wrong. I sent Bobby off to follow the suspect, which by the way, he didn't want to do, and I called you and came up here. So yes, I was worried about you, and, like you said, I freaked a little, but you were so shocked about Denny. I know you aren't involved."

Since she couldn't quite decipher the look on Jen's face, Terri waited for her to continue. "Now, you know. But you weren't quite sure, not a hundred percent." Jen held up a hand when Terri started to say something. "No, I get it. I wasn't honest about this from the beginning. But we have another problem here, Agent McKinnon. Despite all that noise you made to the therapist last week about being all better, you're not really better at all, are you?"

There it was. The question that she didn't want to hear. "No, I guess not." Terri looked down as she crossed her ankle over her knee and began to fiddle with the hem of her jeans. "I'm sorry, Jen. I don't know what to say."

Jen reached across the desk, took Terri by the chin, and lifted her head. "Baby, look at me. We talked about this. I thought you trusted me."

"I do trust you."

Terri saw Jen's agitation in the set of her jaw and the flash of anger that narrowed her eyes. Jen pulled her hand back and crossed her arms over her chest. "Right. And so the first time something bad happens, you're all over me. What the fuck in that says anything about trust?"

Terri stood up quickly and backed away. She needed some room to think. "Jen, this isn't about trust."

"What is this about then?"

"This is about me being scared, okay? This is about me

freaking out and inventing dangerous scenarios in my head simply because someone that you happen to know might be in a lot of trouble." She kept talking, trying to piece together her thoughts out loud, attempting but failing to remain calm. "Yes, I did have a flash that you might know something about this, but that disappeared as soon as I realized that I was right back in the front yard of your old house, watching Davis threaten you. By the time I figured out what was really going on, I was shaking Bobby off the front of my jacket and begging him to let me go."

Jen leaned forward in her chair. "So why didn't you stop when he told you to stop?"

"Because I wanted... no, because I needed to see you. I needed to touch you, to know that you were okay." Terri had never felt as small as she did at that moment, revealing the depth of her fears, the full extent of her loss of control. She turned away toward Jen's bookshelves and pushed back the tears that threatened to spill at any moment. She heard Jen get out of her chair and then felt a tentative hand on her shoulder. Terri turned to face her and the pained look on Jen's face was all it took to reach her tipping point. The tears began to fall. "Jen, what am I supposed to do now?"

"You're supposed to let me in, let me help you. We touched on this that night on the kitchen floor. You need to stop being Agent McKinnon, mighty defender of the universe, and start being just plain Terri, a smart, wonderful, stunningly beautiful, yet imperfect woman who, by the way, has a really goofy computer geek who's madly in love with her. You have to stop trying to be something that we both know you aren't. You aren't perfect, baby, and you can let me help you."

Terri felt the tears flowing freely down her face. God,

she hated crying. She didn't quite trust her voice yet, so she let herself be wrapped up in a bone-crunching hug. She buried her face in Jen's shoulder and accepted the comfort even as it annoyed her that she needed it so badly. When was it that she had become Agent McKinnon, crybaby? She needed to suck it up and get back to work. She sniffed back the last of her tears and tried to put her game face back on. "So, what now, Dr. Rosenberg?"

"First, we need to clean you up. Denny will be here soon, and I assume you still need to talk to her. Do you want me to stay for that?"

"Yes, I think it will put Denny at ease, and I may be able to get more out of her."

"Second, there's obviously still a lot that you and I need to talk about. Can we agree to continue this later? I really don't want to let it drop. I'm worried about you." Terri hesitated, but finally nodded. "I mean, is it okay for you to be out there with a loaded gun strapped onto your belt, and is it also okay that I just said something really close to strap-on and my completely perverted brain took a huge left turn and went somewhere oh-so-very interesting, yet totally unrelated to this discussion?"

"Well, yeah, that's always okay. We can continue this discussion later. I promise."

"Good. Third, you call Bobby and find out where he is and what you need to do to catch up with him."

"That's worked out. Well, sort of. I'm supposed to call him at four. I'm hoping he will have found something out about the woman on the motorcycle. Then maybe you can take me to wherever he is, and no one will have to find out that I took off the way I did."

"Okay. That's good. I can do that." Jen stepped back and reached across her desk to the box of Kleenex that she kept on the computer stand. "Here, you might need these."

Terri chuckled a little as she wiped her eyes with the offered tissue. "Yeah, that might be a good idea. We don't need Denny thinking that the FBI is populated with a bunch of weepy girls. Doesn't do a lot to project an image of confidence, you know?"

"No, it really doesn't."

"There's something else. I can see it all over your face. Tell me."

Jen picked up and began to fiddle with a paper clip. "Yes, okay. There is one more thing. Do you think you should recuse yourself from this case? Maybe you're right. Maybe Denny is too close to me. I'm more than a little concerned about your objectivity here."

"Well, Dr. Rosenberg, isn't that a great question? I wish I had a great answer. Right now, I should probably be thinking about what I'm going to say to fix this with Bobby and we should report in about what's going on. My biggest concern, outside of what we just talked about, is Denny and what's going on with her. I mean, there's still the woman breaking into her apartment, and depending on what she's been hacking into and how far into it she is, she could be facing some criminal charges herself."

"I get that, but what about you?"

"What about me? I might be the only thing between your graduate assistant and three to five years in a federal prison. As Agent McKinnon, mighty defender of the universe, and by the way, I like the sound of that way more than I probably should, I should be taking her into custody to at least investigate what's going on." Jen started to interject, but Terri stopped her with a raised hand. "But I think she just screwed up, is in way over head, which she probably doesn't even realize, and that we should at least get her side of the story. Maybe there's something I can do to help her."

Jen opened her mouth to answer, but never got any words out before there was a knock at the door. She looked toward Terri, mouthing a quiet question, "Are you ready for this?"

Terri nodded yes even though she wasn't sure that she was totally prepared. She slipped into agent mode, at least as much as she could muster, and got up from her chair as Jen called toward the door. "Come on in. It's open."

The door opened slowly. Denny peeked around the doorframe, stopping abruptly when she noticed that Dr. Rosenberg wasn't alone. "Is it a bad time? I can come back..."

"No, Denny. Come on in and have a seat."Jen motioned toward Terri, who was now half-sitting on the edge of the desk. "You remember Agent McKinnon?"

Denny looked a little scared, but Terri could tell, from her years of experience, that the look most likely came from uncertainty rather than full-blown fear. She would have to be careful; she didn't need to try to talk down a panicky college student. She smiled, a look that she hoped would provide a little comfort, as she offered a greeting, "Denny. It's good to see you again."

Denny appeared to relax a little as Jen offered her the chair next to the desk. She came into the office, closing the door behind her, and sat down as requested, still looking more than a little unsure of herself and the situation. Terri didn't move from her perch on the edge of the desk, trying to read Denny's body language to determine the best way to start the conversation. She decided that a gentle line of questions would work better than an outright accusation.

"Denny, is everything all right with you?" Denny only nodded as Terri noted that her demeanor hadn't really changed at all, so she pressed on. "Is there anything going on? Something you should tell us about?"

Terri could almost see the wheels turning in Denny's head as she offered up a response. "I'm not sure what you mean."

Taking a deep breath, Terri realized that the gentle approach would have to be amended. She also realized that she'd have to do it carefully. "Denny, do you have any friends who have a key to your apartment? Maybe a friend who likes to wear leather pants and who also rides a motorcycle?"

That did it. Terri could plainly see the shift in Denny's demeanor. She was scared, as evidenced by the panicked change to her facial expression. Denny shifted her gaze to the floor and nodded almost imperceptibly. "Yes, that would be Faith."

Terri looked over toward Jen, noting that Jen looked a little scared herself, perhaps coming to the full realization that Denny really was in trouble. Turning back toward Denny, Terri asked, "Does she have a key to your apartment?"

Denny, who was still staring at the floor, shook her head no.

"Denny, look at me," Terri said. Denny looked up. "Listen, I'm not here to get you into trouble. I'm here to see if I can help you. I need to know what's going on in order to do that."

"I guess it started a few weeks ago. I got this weird phone call with a job offer, and it concerned me a little. That's when I came to you." She looked toward Jen. "Then she called me back. I told her no, but she pushed a little harder, and offered me more money. It was a lot of money, and I really needed it, so I told her that I'd take the job." She stopped and looked back toward Jen, defending herself as best she could. "I mean, I did listen to you, and I did say no, but..."

Jen answered, "Denny, it's okay. I get it. I was there once and I said yes too. And, if you remember, I told you that it didn't work out so well."

"Yeah, I remember, but it was a lot of money, and so I just—"

Terri interrupted. "Denny, it's okay. I get it too, and I'm not here to judge you about your choice. I need to know exactly what she wanted you to do."

"She wanted me to hack into some giant corporate server. I had an information sheet with a lot of details about some kind of alternative fuel development in Africa. I got partway into the information, and I found lots of weird stuff."

"What kind of weird stuff?"

"Well, there was lots of stuff about all these nasty diseases. You know, like Ebola, and bubonic plague, stuff like that. It scared me, so I called Faith and told her about it. She came over right away, explained it, and convinced me not to worry about it."

"Convinced you? What did she say to do that?"

Denny didn't answer, well, not out loud anyway. Terri watched as Denny turned bright red and lowered her head to stare at the floor again. Jen jumped in. "Denny what happened?"

Again, Denny didn't answer. Jen was not about to let it go, evidently."Denny, did you sleep with her?"

Terri arched an eyebrow, but she held back judgment, waiting to see if Denny responded. After a moment's hesitation, she did answer, very quietly. "Yes."

With no idea what to say next, Terri stopped to think about Denny's revelation. She didn't have to wait long to see what happened as Jen offered up a statement. "Denny, please remember, we're here to help you. Besides, who hasn't had sex with the wrong person at least once? Well, besides Agent McKinnon. She's never done that. I'll shut up now. Sorry, Terri." Terri brushed off Jen's statement with a slight wave of her hand and continued her questioning, "Right. Whatever. Anyway, what happened next?"

"Well, since I couldn't download the file, I told Faith that I'd call her when I was able to. I managed that this morning, and I called her on the way here. I got her voice mail, so I have no idea what's supposed to happen next. I guess she'll want to come to my house later."

"Actually, Denny, she's already been to your apartment, and apparently she didn't find what she was looking for." Denny said nothing, but she did look surprised. "We, the FBI that is, have been following your friend around for a few days. I'm not sure why, but I have a better idea now. Earlier this afternoon, we followed her to your house. That's why I asked you about giving her a key. It would seem that she broke into your apartment and pretty much tore it up looking for something. Do you know what was she looking for?"

Denny said nothing as she reached into the front pocket of her backpack and pulled out a small USB drive. She held it out, offering it up to Terri."I think she was probably looking for this. She gave it to me for when I downloaded the files she wanted."

Terri accepted the offer of the small USB drive, turning it over in her fingers as she attempted to ascertain her next move.

"So what's on this?"

"I'm not sure 'cause I haven't read the entire document. Honestly, it kind of scared me, so I just called Faith and left a message. I figured that she'd know what it was, and I really just don't want to know if it's something awful."

Terri turned the USB drive over, debating her next step. Jen held out her right hand and said, "Why don't we just see what's on that puppy? Might help."

Terri handed her the drive as Denny continued to stare at the floor. Jen slid the drive into an appropriate port on the side of her laptop and waited for the computer to recognize the hardware and load the document. A couple of quick strokes and a click or two to the touchpad opened it. Jen got up from her seat behind the desk and offered it to Terri, who began to scroll through, quickly scanning the document. A nervous silence hung in the office as Terri looked over the file, finally stopping at a spot that captured her attention.

"Holy shit," Terri said into the air, recognizing something that scared her more than a little. Pointing at the screen, she turned to Denny. "Do you know what this is?"

Denny, who was still staring at nothing on the floor, looked up toward Terri and shook her head. "I have no idea what any of that stuff means. It looked scary, so I didn't read all of it."

"What is it?" Jen asked.

"Well, I'm no expert, but this looks like some of the stuff that we saw in our Homeland Security briefing last year."

"Homeland Security? What does this have to do with them?"

"Bioterrorism, Jen. This looks to me like someone is cooking up something really scary that some crazy idiot somewhere can dump into a reservoir. This is bad."

Jen responded, directing her statement toward Denny. "Agent McKinnon has a gift for understatement. I don't think bad begins to cover it, do you, Denny?"

"No, not really. Wow, I really fucked up, didn't I?"

"No, actually, this might be just what I need to help you. Since you found this, we can treat it like an anonymous tip, well, except it's not really anonymous." Terri explained, as the puzzled expressions remained locked in place. "You know, since you brought this to the FBI, in a manner of speaking anyway, we can probably use that to take some of the heat off of your hacking activities."

"Really? That would be cool," Denny brightened a bit.

"Yes, really. I can take this to my boss, and—" Terri stopped mid-sentence as her earpiece crackled to life. Surprised to hear Bobby's voice, she answered, speaking into the microphone attached to her watch. "Bobby? Where are you?"

"Well, actually I'm on campus, in the faculty parking lot across the street from the library. I'm out of the truck and following the suspect. She's on the front steps of McKinley Hall, smoking a cigarette. Is that close to where you are?"

"Oh, shit. That's exactly where we are." Terri turned to Denny. "This Faith person is right outside." She waited while Jen and Denny took in this new information and tried to come up with something to say. Denny offered nothing except a terrified expression, while Jen broke the silence with a question, pointing toward the computer for emphasis.

"We can't let her have that information, right?"

"No, that's not even an option. But here's the best I can come up with. Jen, is there a back door to the building?"

"Yeah, there's a loading dock out the back."

"Okay, what we do is this. I'll head out the back door. Faith is less likely to notice me if I don't come out the front door. I'll meet up with Bobby and we'll get back in the van and follow her. Next, Denny needs to call Faith."

Denny looked panicked.

"It'll be okay," Terri assured her. "So, Denny calls Faith and tells her that she has a meeting off-campus with her professor. That's you, by the way," she said to Jen."

"Well, yeah, I kind of assumed that. What then?"

"Hang out here for half an hour or so, then head out and take Denny with you. I don't think she will wait around for you, at least not conspicuously. She doesn't exactly blend in on this campus, and I doubt she wants to be seen. I think the best plan is to just take Denny to our house. Bobby and I get relieved at six, so depending on where we are at that point, I should be home by seven, seven thirty at the latest. I'll bring Bobby with me, and we can move on from there."

Denny still seemed unsure, so she held up a hand. "Um, Agent McKinnon? What if she follows me to your house? I figure she must want that drive pretty bad if she broke into my apartment looking for it."

Terri tried to offer what little comfort she could. "Well, Bobby and I will be following her, so if she tries something aggressive, we can take care of her then. I'm hoping that if she sees you with someone else that she'll just back off and try to meet up with you later. Sound okay?"

Denny agreed and Terri turned her attention toward Jen. "How about you? Can you do this?"

"Pfft, piece of cake." Terri watched Jen's bravado fade as

she added, "I mean, you'll be right behind us, right?"

"Yes, we'll be right behind if she follows you." She stopped and spoke into the microphone on her watch. "Bobby, did you get all that?"

"That's an affirmative, Agent McKinnon. I'm parked behind the library, so head on over that way and we'll get ready to go."

"Understood." Terri checked around the room to make sure everyone was on the same page. "Okay, Denny. Make your phone call and I'll head out the loading dock." Terri got up, slid the USB drive into the pocket of her jeans, and reached around Denny to retrieve her jacket from the back of the chair. Shrugging back into it, she spoke quietly toward Jen, "I'll see you at home." She started toward the door, but turned back and stopped, adding a small, "Thank you."

Jen answered with a slightly puzzled look on her face. "For what?"

"For always being there for me." She offered Jen a small kiss on the cheek, which was returned with a warm smile. "I'll see you both at home."

She pulled the office door closed behind her, leaving Denny to her task, as she headed out the back door to try to fix things with Bobby.

CHAPTER FIFTEEN

Faith snapped her phone closed, and for the second time in the last two hours, she was pissed about the call. Denny was unavailable for a while, but she had ended the conversation with, "Maybe when we're done, I'll give you a call. It might be late though." Faith had assured her that the late hour was not an issue, but there was something else. Something that Faith had heard in Denny's voice. She sounded nervous. Yeah, that was it. Denny was scared, but she wasn't sure why. Denny hadn't seemed nervous the last time they talked. Actually, she pretty much only seemed brainless and well fucked, but that was different from this.

Faith opted to stop musing in her head. "Nothing I can do, right?" She sat down on the steps of the building and lounged back on her elbows, then sat back up, digging in her pocket for another Marlboro. It was a nice warm afternoon, and she really didn't have to be anywhere. Plus, there were plenty of college kids to watch to pass the time, so there was no rush. Maybe Denny would happen along, and she could get all this over with and get paid.

She took a long drag off her smoke and watched the students walk by. They were a colorful bunch, all decked out in their primary colored T-shirts from wherever you went these days to buy a new shirt that looked old, and what the fuck? Doesn't anyone own a real pair of shoes? Well, flip-flops are cheap, so that could be explained. She made a mental list, dividing the students into three groups for easy sorting. One, there were the brand name kids who shopped at the mall. Their colorful T-shirts had the name of the store emblazoned all over the front. Two, there was the Old Navy crowd, similarly dressed, but the store logo told Faith they were probably on scholarship or had loans to their eyeballs, so mall shopping wasn't on their list of things to do. The third group cruised along in raggedy-bottomed jeans and sweatshirts, looking like they had just rolled out of bed. She bet they smelled like a distillery too.

"Hold on. What's this?" she said as she sat up to watch someone that didn't fit any of her three lists.

Faith took a quick mental inventory of the, wow, the gorgeous babe in the leather jacket. Actually, it was the only leather jacket, well, besides her own that Faith could see. "Black leather, standard button-fly blue jeans, fabulous ass, black shoes... wait..." Faith looked all over the campus. Lots of flip-flops with a decent pair of running shoes mixed in here and there, but no black shoes. Wait, not only black shoes, but black oxfords. Who was this? Faith spoke, softly so no one else could hear as the woman with the chocolate brown hair walked past her. "Turn your head, hot stuff. Let me see your face."

As if the gal in the leather jacket could actually hear, she turned her head in Faith's direction, revealing exactly what Faith expected she would see. A pair of $200 Ray-Ban sunglasses.

That wasn't a college student.

"That's a cop, maybe even a Fed," Faith spoke to herself again. No matter how much they tried not to look like cops, she could always spot one. Just fucking great. "Well, let's just see what that's all about."

Faith took one last drag off her cigarette and flicked the butt out into the middle of the sidewalk, offering a quiet, yet insincere "oops" to the two frat boys that she'd almost hit as they jumped aside and glared at her. She got up, straightened her jacket, and began walking in the same general direction as the cop, heading toward her motorcycle that she'd left parked illegally in the faculty parking lot.

***

Terri's earpiece came to life as Bobby checked in.

"Terri, if you read me, signal, but do not reply."

As requested, Terri pulled her left hand out of the pocket of her jacket and offered Bobby a subtle thumbs up, held close to the front of her body.

"Roger that. Terri, she's up and right behind you. Head into the library so I can see where she's going."

Terri made a quick right turn and ran up the steps to the front of the library. Another dozen or so strides and she pulled open the door of the building, quickly scanning the area for a place where she could look outside and not be spotted. A Ficus tree right next to the door was the closest thing to cover that Terri could find. She ducked behind the large potted plant and signaled Bobby.

"What's up? Why did you want me to come in here?"

"Just a hunch. I watched Ms. Slutbomb cruise you as you passed her, and I wanted to see if she was actually following you."

"Cruise me? What are you talking about?"

It didn't take Terri long to notice that Faith kept walking past the library, apparently not following anyone. She pulled a branch out of the way in order to keep an eye on her.

"Yes, Agent McKinnon, cruising you. Her attention never left your butt as you passed her. You turned in her direction, and then she got up and followed. She's still on the move, so maybe she's headed to her bike. Come on out, I'll meet you on the north side of the building and we'll head back to the loading dock. I'm parked back there."

"Roger that." Terri scooted out from behind the Ficus, pushed open the closest door, and stepped out into the bright sunshine. She spotted Bobby towering over a boxwood hedge and waving to her. It had to be tough to be sneaky when you were six foot five and built like a linebacker.

Bobby gestured toward Faith crossing the faculty parking lot. "Keep an eye on her while I go get the truck. I'll be back in a minute. Hey, you're okay, right?"

"Yeah, Bobby, I'm fine. Sorry about all that back there, but I got a lot of information. I'll tell you everything when we're back in the truck."

Terri watched Faith pull on her helmet, climb astride the bike, and twist the key to start it up. Once Terri heard the engine, she slid out from her spot on the side of the library, and started to make her way toward the back of the building. Removed from her vantage point, Terri could only hear what was going on, quickening her pace as she heard Faith pull the bike out and gun the engine to roar toward the exit of the parking lot. Terri broke into a run toward the van as Bobby backed it out, turning it to bring the passenger side door to bear, offering her direct access. She yanked the door open and jumped in, feet barely clearing the ground as Bobby threw the transmission into drive and gave the truck some gas.

Bobby pulled around the side of the building and into the parking lot. Terri shrugged into her seat belt, juggling the receiver in her lap as she tried to get organized. Faith leaned the motorcycle hard to the left, cutting off a guy in a silver Honda Civic, who honked his horn and flipped her off. Bobby waited for the Honda to get moving again, pulling the van in behind him on Nebraska Avenue. Terri checked the receiver, noting that the transmitter on the bike was still working. "She's heading for the circle. Stay with her."

"I'm on it, Terri. Where do you suppose she's going?"

"I have no clue. Where do you think she's going?"

Bobby shrugged and kept driving, his knuckles white on the steering wheel. Terri knew that the slow pace of the Honda in front of them frustrated him, but he focused on traffic as she watched the receiver in her lap. According to the GPS map on the receiver, Faith had entered Ward Circle, following the counterclockwise loop, eventually making the right turn to get onto the main drag, Massachusetts Avenue. The motorcycle was increasing the distance between them, so Terri urged Bobby on.

"Bobby, she just made the turn for Massachusetts. You need to smoke this guy in the Honda."

"I know that, Terri. Just watch the receiver, okay?"

She was a little surprised by his terse reaction, but waved it off. "Sorry, Bobby. Just drive."

She held on tight to her seat belt as Bobby turned the van hard to the right, skirting in between the Honda and the curb. His actions were greeted with a honk of the horn, and as Terri noted in her side view mirror, another extended middle finger from the understandably agitated Honda owner. Once clear, Bobby could follow traffic around the circle and make the right onto Massachusetts.

The speed of the traffic limited Bobby's progress, but Terri quickly noted that it would be a similar concern for Faith. She was so engrossed with her musings about traffic lights that she almost missed it when Bobby started talking again.

"Sorry about the... you know, the snapping at you thing back there," Bobby said quietly as he slowed the van to stop behind a short line of cars, waiting for the light to change.

"What? Oh, no big deal. What's up with that?"

As the light turned green, Bobby craned his neck in an apparent attempt to look for the motorcycle, and started driving again. "Just... well, this whole thing is getting a little intense, and I'm worried about you." She started to interrupt him, but he held up his hand to stop her. "I know, we can have this whole big heart to heart over a beer sometime soon, but you...Terri, I thought you were done with the whole girly freak out thing."

"Hey," she shot back, a little miffed. "I wasn't being girly. I was concerned." She looked down to check the receiver one more time, noting that Faith was still headed toward the downtown.

"Concerned? You looked positively frantic." Bobby kept driving, giving the van a little more gas to squeak through the intersection at the National Cathedral on the yellow light.

"I thought you wanted to talk about it later."

"Fine, whatever. Later is good. Tell me what you found out from Jen's grad assistant."

"It was just like I thought. The babe on the bike, her name is Faith, by the way, hired Denny to hack into something. Denny got the goods this morning, but had to leave for class, so she called Faith on the way. I guess she decided to take a chance and look for the information while Denny was gone."

Bobby looked around to get his bearings and slowed down a little as he entered the short loop in front of the Naval Observatory. "So what was she looking for?"

Terri shifted in her seat and pulled the USB drive from her pants pocket. "She was looking for this." She held the drive up high enough so Bobby could see it without the risk of sideswiping any parked cars. "And there's some serious shit on here, believe me."

"What kind of shit?"

"The kind of shit that the Homeland Security people showed us last year. There's a bunch of stuff on here about third world diseases and what looks like a recipe to cook up some kind of nightmarish bioterror soup."

"What?" Bobby shot back. "Bioterror soup? What the fuck are you talking about?" He slammed on the brakes as he mistimed the yellow light and had to stop.

Terri put a hand out to brace herself, juggled the receiver, and said, "Easy there. We've still got her on the GPS."

"Yeah, but bioterror soup? God, doesn't anybody just make chili anymore?"

"I promise that I'll make you a pot of chili, but we might want to stay on Faith for a while first."

"Okay. Good idea, but I'm going to hold you to that pot

of chili."

Terri watched back and forth between the GPS receiver and the road, as Massachusetts opened from two lanes to four lanes, allowing for the greater traffic demands of Embassy Row. Faith continued her beeline down Massachusetts, headed back toward Dupont Circle. Bobby's focus on his task allowed Terri a couple of minutes to contemplate Faith's destination. Maybe she was just going back into town, or back toward her starting point in Southeast. Speculation without information always struck Terri as an exercise in futility, so she gave up wondering and returned her attention to the road and all of the brightly colored flags flying from the embassies lining both sides of the street.

Terri checked the GPS. Nothing different, but as she looked up, she could see Faith changing lanes, and mentioned it to Bobby. He waved it off. "She's been doing a little of that, but I think she's just impatient. It's easier to see her since the lanes opened up."

Terri understood impatience. She was feeling a little of that herself, and Bobby's continuous drumming on the steering wheel told Terri that he was reaching critical mass as far as his own impatience was concerned. They cruised steadily toward Dupont Circle and points yet unknown.

Looking down as they passed over Rock Creek Parkway, Terri longed to make the stop at home. She was sick of the van, fatigue and impatience were taking their toll on her mood, and she really just wanted the day to be over. Traffic inched along, and they followed like lemmings. Since they were about a quarter-mile behind the motorcycle, Terri turned her attention to the receiver as Faith turned right into Dupont Circle.

"She's in the circle, Bobby, and looks like she's...oh, wait.

She just made the right onto Connecticut. Where the hell is she going?"

"I am so ready to be done with this shit. The slutbomb on the bike, the traffic, and it's..." He hesitated, checking his watch. "Great, it's almost four thirty and we're on a path for Connecticut Avenue during rush hour. That's just fucking great."

"I'm right there with you, Bobby."

As they pulled around the edge of the circle and made the right onto Connecticut, Terri could see brake lights up ahead, a line of three or four drivers forced to slow as Faith applied her own brakes, slowing just enough to make a right turn. Terri checked the GPS to note the street, pointing it out to Bobby as they approached.

"Bobby, four streets up, turn right."

"But that's a one-way street. That crazy bitch just went the wrong way down a one-way street. What the fuck?"

"Well, according to the tracer, she took that right, then a left after a block and now she's slowing down. Maybe that's where she's going to stop. Head onto the next street that goes the right way, and make your turn."

Bobby did as instructed, turning right at the next corner. He proceeded slowly down the quiet residential street, Terri urging him to go even slower as he approached a four-way stop at the next cross street. She checked the receiver again, but quickly raised her head as Bobby asked, "What the hell is she doing?"

"What?" Terri stopped and stared, unsure of what to think about what she was seeing. "Oh, shit."

There on the corner, sitting on the bike, with one foot on the ground to keep it upright, was Faith. If it hadn't sounded so completely ridiculous, Terri would have sworn that she was waiting for them. After Faith flipped up the visor of her helmet, she raised her right hand and waved. Just a simple wiggle of the fingers in greeting, but Terri couldn't believe it, as she let her mouth hang open in disbelief. It only got worse. Faith closed the helmet visor, pointed directly ahead with one extended index finger, released the clutch, and took off like a bat out of hell.

Terri looked toward Bobby, the open-mouthed look on his face telegraphing his disbelief at the nerve of this woman. The reality of the situation seemed to take hold, like a kick in the head, Terri urging, "Go, Bobby, go," as he stomped roughly on the gas pedal and squealed around the corner.

"How the fuck...?"

"How should I know? Just don't lose her now. This is bad, Bobby. How did she..."

"I knew it. Shit, I knew it." Terri made a quick visual scan of the next intersection. Faith leaned the bike hard to the left and headed back out the side street toward the rush hour traffic of Connecticut Avenue. Bobby followed, Terri hanging onto the upper bracket of the seat belt to keep from coming out of her seat as a result of the hard left turn.

Terri settled back into her seat as she watched Faith out the front window, leaning the bike hard to the right, totally disregarding the red light, to pull back out onto the main drag. "Shit, Bobby...red light."

"Fuck it," he shot back through clenched teeth. "Hang on."

Terri did just that, again grabbing the seat belt with one hand, bracing herself against the side of Bobby's seat with the other as he slowed enough to make sure that he wasn't going to plow into another motorist. The receiver slid off her lap, forcing Terri to juggle it with her feet as she tried to keep it from crashing into the floorboards of the truck. "You knew what?"

"What?" Bobby answered quickly, never taking his eyes off the road as he changed lanes to stay close to the motorcycle.

"You said that you knew it. What were you talking about?"

"Remember when I had you go into the library. The part when I told you that she was cruising your butt? I was concerned that she was following you, and not just because you have a great butt, which you do, by the way, but that's not the issue."

"What is the issue? Do you think she pegged me as a cop?"

"That's exactly what I think. She was watching the college kids, spotted you, and for whatever reason, decided that you were something she wanted to check out, but not in a good way, you know?"

Terri had no idea what to think about this revelation, other than to be relieved by the fact that Faith seemed more interested in screwing around with, and perhaps losing, the FBI on her tail. That meant that Jen and Denny would have been able to leave and go home stress-free, a fact which made Terri feel immensely better. Not that this wasn't a huge fucking mess, but Jen's safety gave Terri one less thing to worry about.

Her moment of relief was short lived as she noticed the blip on her receiver take a hard left turn several blocks ahead. "She made the left onto K Street."

"Yeah, I'm on it. God, I wish I knew where the hell she was headed." He hit the intersection fast, slowing just enough to make the turn, while Terri silently thanked the light for staying green and held on for dear life. After only five blocks, the blip turned right, making things immensely more complicated.

"Bobby, she turned right on Twelfth, but that's one-way the wrong way. Shit. I think I know where she's going."

"Where?" Bobby asked as he crossed 12th and headed for 11th in order to make a right turn.

"Considering that she stopped to wait for us means that she's aware that we have a tracer on her bike. Metro Center is on Twelfth and it's the height of rush hour. She's got three train lines to choose from and a huge amount of people to get lost in. Plus, it's only two blocks from headquarters, and I think she wants to poke us."

"Crafty bitch." Bobby snarled as he made the turn on 11th in order to circle down and around to get on 12th going the proper direction. "Where is she?"

Terri looked closely at the GPS receiver. "She's stopped on the corner of Twelfth and F Streets. Take a right on F and head that way."

Bobby made the sharp right onto F Street, followed by a second right turn to get onto 12th Street, and pulled to a stop just outside the entrance of the station. Terri spotted the bike, parked illegally on the street. Terri didn't see Faith anywhere, but motion on the receiver drew her attention.

"Shit, Bobby, she has the tracer. She must have found it under the seat before she left the parking lot up at the college. I knew it was taking her too long to get moving again." She tossed the receiver toward Bobby and jumped out of the van, closing the door behind her, talking through the open window on the passenger side. "If that blip goes any direction other than straight ahead, let me know." Before Bobby had a chance to protest, Terri was moving fast, headed directly toward the escalator that led to the tracks below street level.

She ran down the escalator, elbowing her way past people as gently as an FBI agent in pursuit of a suspect could, digging in her pocket for her identification and badge. She hit the ground running, past the ticket machines, and made a beeline toward the stationmaster's glass booth. She skidded to a halt on the grimy brick floor, knocked on the window with one hand, holding her open identification wallet to the glass with the other, and urged the startled guy in the booth to open a ticket gate for her. As she quietly thanked the stationmaster, the closest gate whooshed open, admitting her into the mass of people and convergence of tracks that was Metro Center. She spoke into the sleeve of her jacket as she stopped long enough to look around and see if Faith was anywhere within view.

"Bobby, anything?"

She heard her earpiece crackle, a little noisier than usual, but there was a lot of concrete between her and Bobby. "Negative, Terri. She should be straight ahead, no more than fifty yards from your location. She didn't make any turns that I can see from up here."

"Copy that." Terri answered as she calculated fifty yards in her head. Her trip down the escalator and into the station was perhaps only about half that, and she hadn't made any turns to use the escalators for the Blue or Orange Lines, so Faith had to be on the upper platform for the Red Line. Terri watched over the railing as the Shady Grove train pulled out, but not before depositing a large number of arriving commuters onto the already extremely busy platform. Still no sign of Faith.

It only got worse as the Glenmont train arrived, offering a ride in the opposite direction from the first train, adding more commuters to the throng, as well as a touch of panic to Terri's agitation.

"Bobby, anything yet?"

"Negative. Suspect is not moving."

"Please repeat. Did you say not moving?"

"Roger that, Terri. She's dead center on the platform and not moving at all."

"Understood." Terri finally started moving, walking slowly down the escalator to the upper platform. There were plenty of people on the platform, but one stationary object caught her eye. Terri realized that her worst fears had come true, and that one stationary object made her wonder how the fuck she was going to tell McNally that she had lost the suspect. The damn thing just sat there, taunting her.

One very tiny red blinking light stuck to the rim of a trashcan.

After one last quick glance around the station, Terri plucked the tracer from its resting place and slipped it into the pocket of her jeans. As much as she wanted to, Terri fought the urge to kick the living shit out of the trashcan. Not like it would fix anything, and as mad as she was, she'd probably wind up breaking her toe or something equally as stupid.

***

Faith laughed to herself as she hid behind the biggest guy she could find, watching out the window from the safety of the Glenmont train. That was one very pissed off cop out there doing the traditional dance of frustration. God, that was fun.

It really was too bad about having to ditch the bike, but she had bigger fish to fry. Faith needed to find out exactly who those cops were and why the fuck they were following her. And she had to find out who had tipped them off.

CHAPTER SIXTEEN

Things fell apart, and when they did, it was often difficult to put them back together. Right now, Terri knew this fact better than anyone.

After a short conversation about what they should do next, Terri agreed with Bobby that staying with the motorcycle was probably futile. Since it was parked illegally, the Metro Police would deal with it soon enough, and take it away to wherever it was that they took abandoned vehicles. That left her with the problem of Faith. Rather, it left her with the problem of how Faith managed to elude them, leaving her with no suspect and the even scarier prospect of how to broach the subject with McNally. Pissed would be a gentle term for what she was expecting from her boss. Furious and enraged were probably better words, and Terri didn't want to think about that too much right now. She voiced her concerns to Bobby and came to realize, rather quickly, that furious was a good word to describe his feelings at the moment too.

"Yeah, I told you that McNally would have your head, Terri, and I told you that if this went south..."

"Don't you think I know that?" The van had never felt quite so small and cramped. "I get it. I fucked up."

Terri's admission of responsibility seemed to calm Bobby. He whistled long and low. "Yeah, you did, but I let you go. That makes it my responsibility, too. It's still going to cost you way more than a pot of chili to make this right."

"Yeah, I get that too. I suppose a promise of cornbread with your chili isn't what you're talking about, right?"

Bobby actually managed a small laugh. "No, Terri, it's not. Besides you know as well as I do that cornbread is a given when chili is involved, so no, that's not what I'm talking about at all. What I'm talking about here is deep shit, Terri. You freaked out because of Jen and you bolted on me. In case you haven't noticed, I've been defending you for months. I've had to listen to all the locker room bullshit about 'Defective Agent McKinnon,' and you know what? I'm beginning to think that they were right about you."

She tried to answer, but nothing would come out. The only thing she could do was stare back, dumbfounded, unable to untangle the knot of confusion in her head, and quickly decided that maybe Bobby was right. Maybe she couldn't do this anymore. Maybe she was just one of those people who couldn't mix this kind of business with a personal life. She certainly wouldn't be the first one, but that thought only added to her confusion about what it all meant.

Bobby pulled into the garage and threw the van into park. "So, yeah, we need to talk about that, but right now, we need to go check in, and I have no fucking clue about how to deal with McNally. I don't suppose you have any bright ideas, do you?"

"I'll tell him the truth. All of it. How I argued with you

and took off...everything." She held a hand up as Bobby tried to interrupt, stopping him before he could actually get the words out. "Yes, everything. Including the USB drive and the bioterror shit...all of it."

"Are you sure?"

"No, Bobby, I'm not sure, but what else can I do? This whole mess is complicated enough, and I really don't think that making up some fictitious story is going to help us now, do you?"

"No, it's not."

Terri removed her own sunglasses and met his gaze head-on. "Bobby, this is all on me and that makes it my problem to fix. Not yours. Yes, I know you've been my greatest supporter here in the office, but I can't do this to you anymore. It ends right here, right now." She pulled the handle on the door and climbed out of the van. After reaching across the seat to retrieve her computer bag, she slammed the door and urged Bobby to follow. "Come on...let's get this over with. He can't take away my birthday, right?"

***

"You lost her?"

Terri had been right. The word "pissed" didn't even begin to cover McNally's reaction to her tale about hackers and Kazakhstani terrorists and car chases through downtown traffic. She cringed as he began to change colors, his face becoming the same remarkable shade of scarlet as his tie. "Yes, sir."

"You lost her." Not a question this time, but a simple statement of fact. Terri said nothing. "You took off, she figured out that you were following her, and you lost her." McNally sat down hard in his office chair, removed and tossed his glasses onto the surface of the desk, and glared at Terri in a way that actually frightened her. She was granted a moment's reprieve as McNally turned his attention toward Bobby, simultaneously pointing toward Terri. "And you just let her go?"

"Yes, sir, I did. I just thought—"

McNally held up a hand to silence him. "You know, Agent Kraft, right now I really don't care what you thought." After rubbing his face with both hands, McNally looked straight at Terri. "So what's this information that you found?"

Terri handed over the USB drive, tentatively, and started to explain, "There's some disturbing—"

McNally held a hand up to stop her. "You know something else, Agent McKinnon? I really don't want to talk to you right now either." He practically snatched the drive from Terri's hand and sat back in his chair. "Why don't we do this? I need a full report from both of you. While I would normally need that as soon as possible, I want you both as far away from me as would be reasonable at the moment, and I'm pretty sure you both probably feel the same way. I think you both need a day or two to think about how badly you fucked this up today, so I want your reports on my desk in forty-eight hours, and I don't want to see either of you until then. Understood?"

Disappear for forty-eight hours? What did that mean? Absently, she nodded and saw Bobby do the same.

"Good. Then please get out. Now."

Terri wasn't about to stop and ask any more questions. She turned quickly, reaching for the door, bumping into Bobby in their shared haste to get out of the way of their incredibly pissed off boss. Bobby stepped back, pulling the door open to let Terri out first, and scooted in behind her, pulling the door closed on the way out.

"What the fuck was that all about?" Bobby asked. "We just got handed two free days off, and your head is still attached to your neck. I don't get it."

"I wish I had a clue, but he just gave us an out and I think we should take it. So, why don't you drive me home, I'll feed you, and we can try to sort everything out with Jen and Denny. Sound good?"

"Yeah, Terri, that sounds great. Let's go be lesbians and process everything."

With a fairly forceful smack to Bobby's arm, Terri conveyed her feelings about his last comment. Crossing the hallway out to the elevator, she allowed her thoughts about the day to flow, noticing pretty quickly that things were beginning to tangle up again. She stepped onto the elevator, watched Bobby push the button for the basement parking area, and wondered what the hell was going to happen next.

***

"They lost her?"

Skip couldn't quite believe what he had just been told. As he reclined in the chair of his home office, he shook his head in disbelief. All of Bulldog's assurances of assistance had just flown out the window, and now he wanted to talk. More talk. But not on the phone. What the hell did he find out? More importantly, what would he do with the information?

Since Bulldog wanted to meet "as soon as possible," Skip

prepared to do just that. He considered calling his driver and having the car brought around, but thought better of it. "Better do this yourself, Skip." While he wasn't quite sure what Bulldog was so upset about, besides the miserable failure of the two agents that he'd chosen to trust with a personal task, Skip was well aware that the information that the agents had uncovered wasn't something that his oldest and dearest friend would like.

"It's really too bad, now, isn't it, Bulldog?" Skip reached into the lower right drawer of his desk, pulling out a small box of ammunition and his Glock 29. "This could have been so easy." He loaded ten bullets into the clip, slid it into the small handgun, felt the reassuring click as it locked into place, and stood to slide the small weapon into the back of his khaki pants.

On the way out the door, Skip stopped to grab the keys to his black Porsche 911 and opened the closet to retrieve his black bomber jacket, shrugging into it on the way out the door. One last steak dinner at Artie's would have been a nice way to say good-bye, but sometimes necessity dictated other plans. Business of this nature required privacy, and what better place for that than a nondescript parking garage in the basement of a nondescript office building. The fact that Skip had chosen his biggest competitor's parking garage was simply an ironic touch. Sometimes he really amused himself. He pulled the door to his house closed behind him and stepped out into the early darkness of the chilly fall evening.

The drive from his house in Great Falls to Arlington only took about thirty minutes. Skip contemplated the chain of events that had led to this point. Bulldog's agents had fucked up, but that wasn't of great concern since the bimbo on the bike had eluded them. Good to know that the large sums of money spent to procure her services hadn't been wasted. Faith was as good as her reputation touted her to be. Well, maybe not that good. She had sure fallen for his ruse. Kazakhstani terrorist indeed. He'd managed to make a street-hardened tough-babe-for-hire believe that a simple kid from Oakton, Virginia, was an overseas terrorist. He'd also managed to make the FBI, in the form of his oldest pal, believe that there really was a Kazakhstani terrorist. And he'd been doing that for years. It was fun to fuck with people, wasn't it?

Skip pulled his Porsche off the main road, down the side street, and into the parking garage. A short succession of right turns led him to the third basement level. He spotted Bulldog's little blue Ford immediately, mostly because it was the only car parked on the lowest level of the garage. He pulled past the other car, turning his Porsche into the spot next to the driver's side of the Ford, and killed the engine. He looked over at Bulldog, noticing the furrowed brow that told him that Bulldog was upset. Skip pulled the door handle to get out of his own car, pulled his jacket down to make sure that the Glock was fully concealed, and crossed the space behind both cars to open the passenger door and join Bulldog in the Ford.

As he folded his full six foot two inch frame into the compact car, Skip offered a small greeting, but decided that he was uncomfortable and needed to get this done quickly. "So, Bulldog, what's your big problem?"

"This," McNally answered quickly, holding up the USB drive that he'd been fiddling with. "Skip, my agents got this from a hacker that the motorcycle babe hired to break into your system. What the fuck do you think you're doing?"

"What?" Skip decided that feigned innocence might work.

Worth a try anyway. "What's on there?"

McNally shook his head as he handed the drive to Skip. "Okay, we'll play it that way. Someone in your company has evidently decided that it might be fun to dabble with a little bioterrorism." Skip reacted quickly by pasting a fake look of shock on his face, sliding the drive into his pocket, while McNally talked. "C'mon, Skip. You can drop the surprised corporate mogul thing anytime. I know very well that you are aware of everything that goes on in that company of yours, and I'm sure I don't need to remind you that I'm just as guilty as you are right now. Please don't continue to insult me."

Well, maybe feigned innocence wasn't going to work. "No, Bulldog, you're right. You're involved now, so I should probably just tell you about it. It's like this, plain and simple. Terrorism is hot right now, and there's shitloads of money to be made. So, yeah, I wanted in on it."

Skip could tell, from the look of shock on his old buddy's face, that he had actually surprised Bulldog, who said nothing as he stared out the windshield of the car. "So, Bulldog, what do we do now?"

"We, as you just pointed out, have a huge problem. I can't just let this go, but I'm not sure what else I can do. I can't gag my agents, but I suppose I could lose their paperwork. Shit! Skip, I've always tried to be there for you, but I just don't know what I can do this time. Maybe if you destroy your research..."

Play along, Skip. Say whatever it takes to get out of the car.

"I could do that. I'll tear it all up, I can lose this drive"—he patted his pocket for emphasis—"and we can just let the hacker and the babe on the bike deal with each other."

"I don't know, Skip. There's still Kraft and McKinnon to

worry about. They're going to know that something's up if I don't do anything. You've made a huge mess here, and I just don't know what to do."

Skip reached out a hand and clapped McNally on the shoulder. "You know something, Bulldog? I don't know if the answers are coming tonight, but we'll figure it out. Hey, you never know. I might have an attack of conscience first thing tomorrow morning, walk into your office, and confess everything."

"Yeah, right. And I might sprout wings and fly to the moon. But I think you're right about sleeping on it. Might make more sense tomorrow. So I'll call you around lunch time. I need to get home, and none of this makes any sense right now."

Almost there, Skip.

"Good idea, Bulldog. I need to leave too." Skip pulled the door handle and let himself out of the cramped little Ford. He leaned back into the car for a last word, "It's going to be fine, Bulldog. You know, it always is."

Skip took another look at McNally as he slammed the passenger door. Crossing around the back of the car, Skip reached under the back of his jacket and came around to the driver's side door. He tapped lightly on the glass and waited for McNally to roll the window down, as he slid his Glock out from the back of his pants. "Just one more thing..."

"What's that, Skip?"

As McNally leaned his elbow on the doorframe, Skip reached up, left-handed, offering a companionable squeeze to the forearm. "You've always been a great friend, Bulldog." The warm smile on his McNally's face almost made Skip hesitate.

Almost.

When McNally looked down to turn the key in the ignition, Skip pulled the Glock up level with the side of his head, gently squeezed the trigger, and relieved Bulldog of the problem of what he needed to do next. One more small pat to the forearm with a gloved hand and Skip turned to leave.

That solved part of his problem. He patted the USB drive safely tucked into his pocket and realized that the rest of it could be dealt with tomorrow. He slipped the Porsche into gear, pulled out of the parking space, and left the garage without looking back.

Chapter Seventeen

Terri sat at the kitchen table, waiting patiently while Jen got her a drink from the refrigerator. Despite the jumble of thoughts in her head, Terri's ride home with Bobby had been silent. He had tried to talk to her, but she had deflected the conversation by telling him that she wanted to wait until they got home so she could talk to Jen at the same time and not have to explain everything twice. Explaining it once was going to be hard enough.

Terri looked up as Jen set two bottles of beer on the table. In that one glance, she found everything she needed. Jen's support, trust, love, all of it. Everything she needed to get through whatever it was that the next few hours or days would bring. Despite any misgivings she might have had about Jen's past, Terri knew that this wonderful, goofy person was her rock, and boy, did she need something solid to hang onto right now.

Terri accepted the offered bottle of beer. Jen touched her lightly on the temple. "Still pretty busy up there, isn't it?"

"Yeah, Jen, it is."

As she looked down to pick at the label of her beer, Terri

noticed the hand sliding its way toward her thigh. She welcomed the comforting touch, as Jen asked, "So, you've already told me about the big chase scene. Do you want to tell me what happened in the office? Bobby is out in the other room. It sounds like he's canceling a date with the boy toy *du jour*, so if you'd rather..."

"No, he was there so I'll fill you in. I decided to tell McNally everything."

"Oh, shit. I don't even need to ask if he blew a gasket."

"Yeah, that would be a nice way to put it. But he did the strangest thing, and I'm still trying to figure out what he meant. Not only did he not eviscerate me on the spot, he actually gave Bobby and me two days off to, as he said, think about how badly we screwed up." Terri could see that Jen was just as confused by this piece of information as she was, "Yeah, I'm right there with you, sweetie. He didn't tell us to go look for her, nothing. And I have no clue what that means."

"So, let me get this straight. You've been following someone around for a few days, but you don't know why, right? Then you freak out, run off, and lose her down the Metro. And for all of this, you get two free days off? What the hell does that mean?"

Terri shrugged and tried to answer. "I wish I knew. If I didn't know better, I'd swear he was trying to hide something."

"Are you sure he's not?"

"Jen, this is McNally we're talking about. Mr. Thirty-years-with-the-Bureau, college football hero, ex-Marine, gruff, honest to a fault. That guy?"

"Yeah, but you're the cop. Do the math."

Terri crossed her arms over her chest and offered Jen another puzzled look. "But McNally? I could believe that about almost anyone else, but..."

"Baby, he should have put you back on restriction, no discussion, no questions asked, and you know that as well as I do. I just don't see any other explanation."

"Explanation for what?" Bobby asked as he returned to the kitchen and pulled a beer out of the refrigerator, twisted off the cap, and took a long drink.

"Why McNally didn't rip Terri's head off for freaking out the way she did." Terri shot a quick glance of displeasure toward Jen, who tried to amend her statement to something a little gentler. "I mean, well, you know what I mean."

"Yeah, I know what you mean, and it's okay. You're right, I did freak out, and I should have gotten into trouble for it."

"But hey," Bobby interjected, tone dripping with sarcasm, "we got two days off. Woohoo!"

"Yeah, great," Terri offered in response. "We got two days off, no suspect, our boss is apparently losing his marbles, and we've still got a hacker to deal with." Terri stopped to look around. "By the way, where is she?"

"Oh. Denny," Jen answered after she took another long swallow of beer, "She was still pretty shaky when we got home, so I gave her a beer and set her up with the TV upstairs. Last time I checked, she'd fallen asleep on the sofa watching *South Park*."

"*South Park*?" Terri scrunched her nose in disgust. "Eww."

"What? It's funny." Jen hesitated at the look of disbelief on Terri's face. "Or so I've heard."

Terri arched one eyebrow and put on her best "you're busted" face, and said, her tone low and slightly menacing, "Jen..."

"Okay, I might have seen it once or twice."

Bobby piped in quietly, "I like it. I mean, c'mon. Big Gay Al's Big Gay Animal Sanctuary. That's funny shit."

Jen jumped all over Bobby's comment, as she pointed at him and started to laugh. "Yeah, that was funny. And that weird guy with the puppet?"

"Yeah," Bobby answered, pointing back. "C'mon, Jen, say it with me."

In perfect unison, Jen and Bobby offered up a hearty, "Oh my God, they killed Kenny!" and broke into paroxysms of laughter.

All Terri could do was stare in utter disbelief, as she shook her head and said, "You two scare me sometimes." Her comment was greeted with a chorus of giggles and muttered apologies. "We really do need to figure some things out. Anybody have any thoughts?"

Jen sheepishly raised her hand. "What about Denny?"

"What about her?"

"I mean Faith is gone, right? But does that mean that she's out of the picture? I assume she'll still try to hook up. Well, not hook up as in *hook up* as such, especially considering what Denny told us, but I have to assume that she still needs the USB drive and the information. Is Denny still in some kind of danger?"

"I don't know," Terri answered and looked to Bobby for his opinion. He shrugged in response, letting her know that he was equally clueless, so she began to work the process out loud. "Okay, let's think about this. Faith was willing to break into Denny's apartment and even try to catch up with her at school. When she found out that wasn't going to work, she decided to play with us instead. Agreed?"

Bobby answered, "Yeah, so far so good. Go on."

"And then, we lost her, but we also know that she didn't get the USB drive, because Denny gave it to me. I gave it to McNally, so we know the information is firmly in the hands of the Bureau. Still with me? So, maybe it would be all right if Denny got in contact with Faith again and gave her the information just to tie her officially to the crime. I know we don't have the drive, but it looked to me just like the ones that anyone can buy at Office Depot or Target, right?"

Jen answered."Um, actually, I have one just like it upstairs. It was a Sandisk, one gig, and they were on sale at Staples a couple of weeks ago, so I bought two or three. Just take one of those."

"Two or three?" Terri asked. "How many USB drives do you need?"

"Well, I kind of tend to lose them, so I have a couple, you know, a few, maybe four or five or so, not exactly sure..."

"Jen..."

"Okay, there's eight USB drives in my desk drawer." Jen turned to look at Bobby, offering him a weak smile in a really lame attempt to defend herself."I kind of have a thing for computer stuff and office supplies."

Terri interjected, "Go on, Bobby. Ask her about how many different colored pens she has."

"Hey." Jen defended herself. "Color coding is important, you know?"

Bobby just shook his head. "Sounds a little insane to me, Jen."

"Be nice, Bobby," Terri said, coming to Jen's assistance.

"She prefers the term quirky. But we're getting off topic. Denny has her computer with her, right?"

"Yes."

"Okay, so, she can copy the document to the drive, call Faith, and just give it to her."

Bobby jumped in. "Ooh, then we can follow Denny and get Faith back at the same time. Well, not actually get her back, but we can at least see where she goes after she meets up with Denny and maybe even follow her to meet up with the guy from Kazakhstan. Oh, Terri, do you still have that tracer that you picked up in the Metro?"

Terri checked her pockets for the tracer. "Yes, I do." She pulled it out and set it on the table. "But we don't have the receiver, so it's not much good."

"Ah, but we can get one," Bobby answered. "We can call the new guy in supply and check one out. I'd better be the one to call him though, right, Terri?"

Terri looked away sheepishly, prompting Jen to ask, "Do I even want to know why you can't call the supply guy?"

"Remember last winter, right before we came down to your house, when I yelled at the new guy in the office and told him to go fetch me coffee? Yeah, well, it's the same guy. He transferred down to supply, and he's still kind of afraid of me."

"He thinks she's nuts, Jen."

"Thank you so much for that, Bobby. Whatever. Why don't you go call him right now and see what he has to say?"

Bobby went out into the dining room to make his call, giving Terri a few minutes alone with Jen. "Do you think Denny would be willing to do this?"

"Honestly, baby, I think she's so freaked out at the moment

that she'd probably do anything just to make sure that it's really over, you know?"

"Yeah, I get that." The last thing she needed to do right now was go off half cocked and try to chase down Faith, but McNally's odd behavior really left her, and Bobby for that matter, with little else in the way of options. Of course, the whole operation could become problematic depending on Faith and if she had figured out why the FBI was following her.

Terri stopped musing long enough to recognize Jen's hand on her arm, offering that same comforting touch that Terri so desperately needed.

"Terri, are you sure about this?"

"No, Jen, I'm not, but I have no idea what else to do." Terri leaned forward with her elbows on her knees, rubbing small circles at her temples to keep the frustration-fueled headache at bay. It wasn't working. "I suppose we could call McNally for approval, but that means we'd have to give Denny up, and since we lost Faith in the Metro, it all falls on Denny. I'd hate to see her become the sacrificial lamb in all this mess, but if McNally is hiding something, he won't hesitate to do that. And since this is all my fault—"

"Baby, stop. This isn't all your fault."

Jen pulled at Terri's hand, losing the grip quickly as she gave into her frustration and stood up, almost knocking her chair over in the process. "Then whose fault is it, Jen? Tell me."

Jen stood to approach, but Terri kept her at a distance, raising her hands to push back if necessary. The tension in the room became palpable as Terri tried think clearly and keep the demons at bay long enough to try to make sense of what was happening to her. That wasn't working either.

"Jen, I screwed everything up because I freaked out. If I would have stayed with Bobby and just called you, we wouldn't have lost Faith, and we wouldn't be sitting in the kitchen now, waiting for pizza, cooking up all this half-crazed bullshit. Bobby and I would have gotten relieved, and we could have come home, he could have gone on his date, and none of this would have happened."

Jen tried to step closer, but Terri's agitated demeanor held her back. "Okay, yes, that would have all been fine and dandy, but now you have reason to suspect that your boss was using you for something weird, and that there's some crazy asshole out there cooking up something to kill us all, which, by the way, I think we should all be glad that you found, so a great big woo and hoo for that, and you might just be keeping some poor kid, who deserves nothing more than a swift kick in the pants for being stupid, out of prison."

Jen tried to approach again, this time with a little more success as Terri relaxed her shoulders and allowed Jen to take her by the hands. "Yeah, I suppose."

"Yeah, you suppose is right." Jen visibly brightened. "Hey, and we also found out that my completely insane office supply habit might just save the world from some really ugly biological apocalypse, so we're all good here. Right?"

Terri warmed to the realization that no matter what happened, even when she was at her worst, that she was never going to be in it alone, as long as she had Jen. That was a nice thought to have. She sniffed a little and wiped at her eyes. "Yeah, you're right. I still think we should call McNally and—"

"Belay that, Agent McKinnon." Bobby was back, finished with his phone call, and apparently bringing news. "I think the last person we need to talk to right now is McNally. I talked to your little buddy, Newbie, down in supply, and it would seem that everything we've been doing for the last week never happened. There's no record of any of it. No requisitions, no case numbers, nothing. I don't know how he did it, because, God knows, we need a requisition for toilet paper in the men's room, but McNally managed to keep two teams of agents fully outfitted for surveillance for close to a week, and there's not one shred of anything documenting any of it."

Terri could not believe what she was hearing, "What?"

"You heard me. Nothing, nada, zilch. No wonder he wanted us out of the office."

"Yeah," Terri answered as she kept trying to make sense of this last little revelation in her head. Nope, wasn't working this time either. "Jen, you were right and I still have no idea what that means."

Bobby piped in, "Oh, but wait. It gets better. No one can find McNally now. He's not at work, he's not at home, and he's not answering his cell phone."

Terri didn't even attempt to ask if anyone else was as clueless as she was at the moment. The dumbfounded expressions on their faces told her all she needed to know. Now what?

***

Faith paced and chain-smoked around the tiny efficiency apartment that she had rented to serve as a home base for the duration of the job. The voice on the other end of the phone continued to piss her off, more and more, actually making her contemplate asking for more money. It was, of course, a ridiculous notion since it was now obvious that the cops were on to her, and that fact had a tendency to make people tight with their money. She still wasn't sure what kind of cops they were, but considering the advanced electronics, in the form of the tracer she had found under the seat of her bike, they weren't locals. FBI, maybe even Homeland Security. Hell, considering the nature of the information that she had been hired to locate, it could have even been the CIA. Faith just had no way of knowing, and this asshole on the phone wasn't helping. Not a fucking bit.

"Listen, dude, this situation is getting completely out of hand. You said this operation was watertight, and now my hacker is spooked, I've got cops on my ass, and I don't even know who the fuck they are. I'll get your information, but I need something from you, and all this cryptic bullshit just isn't going to cut it."

Continuing to pace like a caged animal, Faith listened as her employer attempted to explain that he had no idea what was going on.

"Not going to cut it, buster. You owe me for the bike, and I should just tell you you're not paying me enough—"

She stopped, interrupted by a warning from the other end of the call.

"Yeah, but I'll get the drive back from my hacker. She may be spooked, but I know how to work her. It just might take a couple more days. I still need you to find out who those cops are and who tipped them off."

She stopped pacing long enough to light another cigarette from the burning end of the one she was currently smoking, stubbing the butt out in the overflowing ashtray. "Then what the fuck good are you? This whole thing just got lots more complicated, and I'm not going to sit here with my thumb up my butt while you hang me out to dry. For all I know, you're getting ready to pack up your dolls and dishes and head back to Whatthefuckistan—"

The voice interrupted her again, which only served to fuel her rage.

"Yeah, yeah, I know. Kazakhstan, whatever. Who gives a shit? Could be Bumfuck, Egypt, for all I care, but that doesn't solve the current problem. There are cops involved now, my transportation is gone, and you're a useless waste of space. Help me out here."

Faith stubbed out the current cigarette she was smoking, fished in her pocket for another one, and pulled out nothing but an empty pack, which she immediately crumpled into a ball and hurled angrily across the room.

"Yeah, ten grand would cover the bike. You going to wire it into my account?"

The voice answered her as she picked through the ashtray looking for a long butt to smoke.

"Well, thanks. That helps. And yeah, I'll get you your information, hopefully by tomorrow night. I'll call you when I'm on the way over to her place."

Faith snapped her phone closed, stopping just short of hurling it across the room too. "Asshole," she muttered again to the closed phone. At least he was going to cover the bike. That helped. She contemplated going out to blow off some steam, but hesitated as she came to the decision to try Denny one more time. She flipped the phone open and scrolled down through her list of contacts, stopping at "Skater Boi," and pushed the call button. Fuck. Voice mail again.

"Denny, Dude, I know it's late, but I still need to talk to you. Call me tomorrow. I'll be out most of the day, but you know the number. Later."

Faith let out a long, frustrated huff of breath. Shit. No hacker, no bike, and no fucking cigarettes. "This sucks," she muttered to herself, as she dug through her pockets for some cash for a taxi. She couldn't do anything about the bike until tomorrow morning, but she could go out, buy some smokes, and deal with the monster-sized case of hungry and horny that all this shit had given her. Too bad about Denny. That would have solved the second part of her little problem quite nicely, but it didn't really matter now, did it?

***

Skip stared at the phone in his hand, muttering softly, "Bitch," as the call was terminated on the other end. Faith really was good at what she did, but she was proving to be as big of a pain in his ass as Bulldog had been. Well, he could fix that problem, too, and most likely the same way.

Much of his problem was already solved. He had removed the USB drive with the files from the hands of the FBI. That part was easy. What wasn't easy was the fact that the drive was only part of the problem. There was still a hacker out there, with his research on her hard drive, and he needed to plug that leak too. It was really too bad that he had lost the free government-sponsored surveillance that he had procured to keep watch on Faith, but she would call him tomorrow. Faith had given him the name of the hacker, and the weird programmer guy that worked in Skip's own Information Systems Department had broken into the American University student database and provided the rest. Maybe he'd just head out that way tomorrow, when Faith was on her way there, and see what he could do about killing two birds with one stone.

"Two birds with one stone." Skip typed the necessary information into his computer to transfer ten thousand dollars into the account that he had set up for Faith. The nice thing about the account was that it was still actually his account, so he could just pull whatever money was left out of the account once Faith was dealt with. Besides, he'd always wanted a motorcycle.

Skip poured himself a glass of twelve-year-old scotch and headed into the media room to find something to watch on television. As the first slug of dark amber liquid warmed his insides, Skip languished in the glow of total control.

Tomorrow. It would all be fixed tomorrow.

CHAPTER EIGHTEEN

Despite the long break that a restless night's sleep had provided, Terri was reticent. Reluctant to share her feelings, she sat back at the kitchen table, ignored her breakfast, and watched while Bobby and Jen tried to cook up solutions to the problem at hand. It was strange, watching the two of them interact like that; making plans over coffee and the doughnuts that Bobby had picked up on his way over. Most of what made it strange was the way Terri felt about the whole situation. None of their ideas sat right with her, because every experience she'd had for the last six months had served to teach her that riding off after babes on motorcycles, or anyone else for that matter, with no support or backup, was a stupid idea at best. And Bobby knew better. Didn't he? Or was he just so completely pissed off about losing Faith and the resultant ass chewing that he had received from McNally, that he was ready to try the cowboy thing himself? Definitely not a good idea, not this time.

And what about Jen? Well, that one was easier to explain. She had a problem to solve and that was what she did best. There were constants and variables at work, and Jen had a better handle on things like that than anyone Terri had ever known before. She loved watching Bobby and Jen together. Jen talked and plotted, waving her hands in the air, and Bobby grabbed Jen's sleeve to keep her hand out of the large coffee cup where she kept a small collection of her beloved colored pens.

She was just about the cutest thing Terri had ever seen. And that made it worse. Business like this, with guns and lies and car chases, wasn't what Terri wanted for Jen. Bobby was a professional. He knew what the job meant, and it was probably why he was still single. Jen wasn't a fed. She deserved her innocence and her USB drives and to watch *South Park* if she wanted (even though Terri, for the life of her, could not understand why), but not this. Terri mused a little more, wondering about Jen's innocence. Yes, there were all the girls when she was younger, and the computer hacking, but the innocence, or lack thereof, that Terri was thinking of was more related to the fact that Jen was the only one amongst them who actually knew what it felt like to have a loaded weapon inches away from her brain with a crazy man at the trigger. Terri shuddered at the thought, a small movement that failed to go unnoticed, as Jen stopped talking to Bobby and asked her a question.

"Terri, baby, are you all right? You're not saying a lot."

Bobby chimed in. "Actually, Jen, she's not saying anything. Terri, are you still with us?"

"Yeah, I'm just thinking too hard, as usual." Terri sloughed off their concern with a wave of her hand.

It didn't appear as though Bobby was buying her excuse. "Terri, you know that if you have a problem with this, you need to tell me." They were both looking at her now.

"Okay, you're right. This whole idea just doesn't work for me. Yes, I want to spare Denny any more problems, but the idea of handling it ourselves strikes me as absurd. Especially considering everything that's ever gone wrong when we've done that in the past."

Terri stopped talking, and looked toward Jen for support. Getting only a small shrug as a response, Terri turned her head and directed her full attention toward Bobby, since he seemed to be the only person with a strong opinion at the moment.

"Terri, think about our options. First, we do have surveillance tapes of Faith, that is if McNally hasn't made those disappear too, but it's all one-sided cryptic conversations. Not a lot to go on, and you know as well as I do that the Federal prosecutor won't touch it. It's too sketchy. Right?"

Reluctantly, Terri had to agree.

"Second, Denny is still crashed out upstairs, so that means we have her computer with the hacked files, but all we have, officially, is her word that Faith hired her, since the video is probably inadmissible. So then we take the info to McNally, or whoever we decide that we can trust, and anyone at the Bureau is going to take one look at the all that bioterrorism shit and call Homeland Security, pretty effectively removing us from the loop, again most likely landing Denny in the women's prison at Alderson, and the place just hasn't been the same since Martha Stewart got out."

"Yeah, but Alderson has a softball team, and..." Jen hesitated as Terri and Bobby stared at her. "What? I know these things."

"Of course you do. Hey, maybe they'll let Denny have a weekend pass to go to the Women's Final Four." Turning her attention toward Bobby, Terri added, "Jen likes the Final Four," turned back toward Jen and added, "don't you, sweetie?"

"Hey, it was just once, well, twice, but...yeah."

"Do I even want to know what the fuck you two are talking about?"

"No," they answered firmly, in unison.

"Well, okey dokey then." Bobby turned his attention back to Terri. "So, can we agree that we really don't want the Homeland guys in on this?

"Yes," Terri answered, and urged Bobby to continue. "Go on."

"Third, we take the George McNally approach, erase Denny's hard drive and pretend like none of this ever happened. Then sometime next week or next month, Faith shows up at Denny's house, demands the information or her money back, Denny has neither, and winds up floating face down in the Potomac. We don't know for sure that that's what will happen, but my guess is that it's at least a possibility, and I, for one, couldn't live with that option."

Terri was, again, forced to reluctantly agree. "No, I couldn't live with that either. So, what does that leave us with?"

Jen motioned to Bobby, indicating that he should explain the plan. "Okay, Terri, we can't get the receiver from supply because of McNally and all his sneaking around. But what we can do is this." Terri followed his glance as he turned toward Jen. "I think Jen can explain this part better than I can."

Jen visibly brightened, eager to explain her part of the plan. "Right. I looked at the tracer and with what Bobby told me, it sounded like a standard GPS transmitter. Of course it's much smaller than the one that I have, but..."

Terri was confused, so she asked, "You have a GPS tracer? Why do you have that?"

"Well, you know. If we ever want to go camping or something like that, and we need to navigate through the woods..." Jen hesitated as Terri began to laugh again. "What?"

"Camping? Yeah, right. You hate camping." Terri turned her attention toward Bobby. "Jen told me once that her idea of roughing it was a Holiday Inn with no hot tub. Right, sweetie?"

"Well, yeah, but...whatever." Turning her attention toward Bobby, she answered, "Yes, she's right. A mini-bar is nice too, but that's not important now. So, to answer your first question, they had this really cool GPS tracer slash software package at Staples once, so I bought it. It is fun to play with on car trips, not that I've taken a whole lot of car trips, well, except for last spring when I was driving back and forth from Harrisonburg to here every weekend, but that—"

"Jen," Terri stopped her. "Focus, sweetie."

"Oh, yes, GPS, right. Anyway, so all I need to do is tweak the software and reset the respondent frequency, and we can use my computer to follow the tracer. It's really no big deal."

"Can you set this up on your laptop so Bobby and I can take it with us?"

"Hmm, I suppose I could do that, but the laptop might not have enough juice to keep up, so the data would be slow, possibly unreliable to the point that you could lose her. The processor on the mainframe upstairs is lots faster, so you'll get actual real-time data that way. You can't take it with you, but I could monitor it and stay on the phone with you."

Terri shook her head emphatically. "No, Jen, I don't want you..."

"Baby, I'll be right here in the house. We lock all the doors, turn off the lights, and I'll keep Snickers close by. I'll be on the phone with you the whole time. You can even take my extra headset so we can just leave the line open. So you'll be on the wire with Bobby, on the phone with me, and we'll have Denny put the tracer in her pocket, or tape it in her bra, or something like that."

Terri still wasn't convinced. She turned her attention toward Bobby. "What do you think? Can we even do this?"

"I don't see why not. I know we're hoping that Denny delivers the goods, Faith takes off, Denny goes home, and that's the end of it. The only part that concerns me is that we lose the tracer on Faith once Denny goes home, but we can always follow her the old-fashioned way and hope that she still thinks she lost us in the Metro."

"But, Bobby, she spotted me coming out of McKinley Hall, and she knew that's where Denny was, so wouldn't she assume that we were there looking for Denny too? I know I would, so we need to be prepared for the worst."

"Oh, oh... I got it." Jen waved her hand as she bounced eagerly in her seat. "That tracer is small enough that I could open up the USB drive and tuck it in there. That way, my computer follows the drive regardless of who has it. Problem solved."

"I'm still not sure." Terri said. "There are way too many variables at work here, and it's a lot to expect from Denny.

"Hey, why don't I just go ask her about it? I can tweak the tracer, show her what's up, and see what she thinks. Can't hurt to ask, right?"

No matter how hard she tried, Terri couldn't figure out a problem with that. "I guess not. It's just that this all feels, I don't know, wrong, stupid, inevitable. I hate it."

"I know, baby, but no matter how many times we go over this, there just isn't a good solution. If Denny goes for it, it may be the only way everyone comes out of this okay. I'll go talk to her."

Terri watched Jen leave the kitchen and then turned to stare out the window at the brightening sky. She could hear Bobby breathing and realized he had stopped inhaling doughnuts and was probably watching her.

"Terri."

She swallowed hard but didn't turn around. "Bobby, do you know what I have always loved about being an agent?"

"What's that, kiddo?"

Terri could hear the sadness and pity in his voice and struggled to talk around the knot in her throat. "The feeling that what I did mattered, that every decision I made helped. I have always been in control. Right and wrong were so clear-cut, and all of that is gone now."

"Terri, look at me."

She did and felt her heart warm. There sat Bobby, all six foot five of him, wearing his heart on his sleeve and powdered sugar on his nose. Terri reached out and brushed the sugar away.

"Thanks, I'm sure you'll take me more seriously now. Damn, I always screw up the big emotional moments. What I wanted to say was—shit!" Bobby reached into his pants pocket for his phone. "It's work. Hang on."

"Terri, baby, come here!" Jen had that "I need you now" tone to her voice.

Terri pushed up from the table and deposited her coffee cup in the sink. As she climbed the stairs, she could hear Jen pacing around above her. That was not a good sign.

"Jen, what's wrong?" Terri asked as she came through the door.

Jen stood in the middle of the media room, holding a single sheet of paper.

"It's Denny...she's gone."

"What do you mean, gone? Where did she go? How?"

The message was short and to the point:

Dr. R,

I'm sorry for this mess and all the trouble I've caused you and Agent McKinnon. I should have listened to you in the first place, but I didn't. So I'm gonna make it right. I heard you all talking, and I know I can do this. I'll give Faith what she wants and the FBI can follow me and catch her. I have to try to clean up the mess I made. I'll call you.

Denny

Terri crumpled the note in her hand. "Well, isn't this just great? What the hell is she thinking? Going out without backup. She could get herself killed."

Terri rounded on Jen, prepared to continue her tirade, but stopped when she saw the terrified look on Jen's face.

"Oh God, I'm sorry, Jen. Come here." She folded Jen into her arms and stroked her back gently. "Sweetie, we'll find her. It'll be okay. We'll call her and go get her before she can get very far. Nothing's going to happen to her. We'll get to the bottom of this and then Faith, her boss, and McNally will all have to answer to whatever it is they are up to."

"Not McNally, Terri."

Between the note and the fact that Jen seemed dangerously close to melting down, Terri hadn't heard him come up the stairs. He stood in the doorway with his cell phone still in his hand and an expression Terri had seen far too many times during her career. In that moment, she knew exactly what Bobby was about to say and closed her eyes in a futile attempt to push it away.

"He's dead. Security guard found his body in a parking structure over in Arlington. Single gunshot wound to the head."

***

"You can do this, Robertson. It's the right thing to do."

Denny spoke quietly to herself as she walked quickly, ignoring her own reflection in the front windows of the shops she passed. Sneaking out the front door had been easier than she had imagined it would be. Apparently, Snickers had been more interested in Agent Kraft and his bright pink box of doughnuts than a half-cocked graduate assistant tiptoeing barefoot down the steps and out the front door. After running around the corner and stopping long enough to slip into her blue suede Vans— *fucking new shoes that I just had to have*—she made her way out toward Connecticut Avenue with the plan of heading toward the Dupont Circle Metro Station and back to her own apartment. She'd call Faith when she got there, and then she'd call Dr. Rosenberg and tell her the plan.

"Make it right, Denny."

Her mother's voice, telling her every time to make it right. Handing her a dollar bill to take to the guy with the three missing fingers who ran the convenience store on the corner. She hadn't really wanted to shoplift the gum, but they dared her. Getting her a legal pad and a pen to write the apology to the coach and the principal. Sneaking beer on the bus to the softball tournament sounded like fun, until they got caught. Pushing her out the front door of their house to go next door and apologize for smashing Marcus Scott's nose all over his pathetic, pimply-ass face. Well, she had only been thirteen and didn't know then that he was right, and besides, even if she was queer, nobody got to call Denny a dyke. Except for Denny.

"Make it right, Denny."

Turning over the USB drive in her pocket, recently liberated from Dr. Rosenberg's desk drawer, a new voice sounded in her head. *"If a crazy person shows up at your house ten years from now and threatens to blow your brains out, you'll really wish you'd listened to me... if you remember, I told you that it didn't work out so well... some poor kid, who deserves nothing more than a swift kick in the pants for being stupid... I don't think bad begins to cover it, do you, Denny?"*

Striding purposefully toward the long escalator at the Metro Station, Denny stopped to respond to a buzzing in the pocket of her cargo pants, looking over her shoulder to make sure that no one was coming after her. Not yet anyway She noted the caller ID. It was Faith.

After offering tentative greeting, Denny listened as Faith began to talk.

"Denny, dude, you've been hard to track down. Everything okay?"

Denny tried hard to keep the fear out of her voice. "Yeah. Sorry about that, but it got late, so I spent the night on Dr. R's sofa. I've got that stuff you wanted."

"Good girl, D. I knew you'd come through. Are you on your way home now?"

"Yeah, I'm on my way down to the Metro right now. Are you coming over?"

"Yes, ma'am. Tenleytown-AU station, right? How about if I meet you there? I'll give you a ride home on the bike."

"Okay. See you in a few." As soon as Faith said good-bye, Denny snapped her phone closed and returned it to the pocket of her khaki cargos. She was going to make it right.

***

Faith closed her own phone, gritting her teeth against the completely uncomfortable sensation of the compact Glock handgun pressed insistently against a spot about an inch below her left ear. "How was that?"

Skip answered in a maddeningly smooth tone that reminded Faith of a used car salesman. "Faith, that was perfect. I'd offer you a hearty round of applause, but you know..." He stopped, mid-sentence, twisting the gun against her neck for effect.

The muscles in her jaw clenched and unclenched as she stared at the back of the limo driver's head. "Yeah, I know."

"Tony. Tenleytown Metro Station, please. Oh, and don't spare the horses."

Faith closed her eyes as Tony pulled the Lincoln away from the curb and headed north, attempting to will away the thoughts about how this was all going to end. The Glock at the base of her skull did nothing to help.

***

Jen paced the route from the sink to the refrigerator and back again for about the twenty-eighth time, clutching her cell phone in her right hand with her arms crossed over her chest, trying to comfort herself. The knot of nerves in her head made her want to cry, and the knot in her stomach made her want to throw up, but she really didn't want to do either, so she just paced like a tiger in a cage. Bobby and Terri sitting there quietly at the kitchen table did nothing to ease her fragile nerves, especially considering that they were both armed, wired for sound, and decked in those spiffy black Kevlar vests. This was just not a scene she had ever wanted to replay, especially considering the first time it had happened in her old farmhouse last winter. She could handle all the plotting and the planning. What she couldn't handle was the waiting, because it was all too familiar. Terri's soft voice pulled her from her musings.

"Jen, sweetie, would you please relax? She said she'd call."

"But, Terri, it's been over an hour. She said she'd call, but she hasn't, and she's not answering her phone. What if something went wrong? What if Faith did something bad? Oh, God, she's probably hurt. Can't someone just go after her?"

"Jen, stop. We don't know where she is, and if we go now, where are we supposed to go?"

Jen tried to think of an answer, but none was forthcoming. So she chose to lean into the embrace that Terri was offering and try to will away the demons in her head. As hard as she tried, she just couldn't shake the picture in her head of Denny, scared out of her wits, pinned against a doorframe somewhere by Faith or a Kazakhstani terrorist with an itchy trigger finger. She was so frightened for Denny that she shook, and the only thing that kept her from coming completely unglued was Terri's arms holding her together. Jen actually let out a yelp of surprise as the phone went off in her hand. She pulled free, and had to take a second to process that it wasn't an actual call, but a text message. "What the hell...?"

"What?" Terri asked quietly.

"Text message...it's from Denny." As she hit the proper buttons to open the message, she saw Bobby get up from his seat at the kitchen table to see what the message was about. She looked at the small screen on her phone, not quite understanding the one word message.

Wrhose.

She held the phone out toward Terri. "Do you know what this means?"

Once Terri and Bobby exchanged what looked like an understanding glance, Jen hoped that they knew what it meant.

"I'm pretty sure that it means warehouse, Jen, and it also means that we have a pretty good idea where she is. It also means that I have to leave. Will you be okay?"

"Yeah, I'll be fine. Please be careful."

"I always am. I love you, you know?"

"Yeah, baby, I know that. I love you too." Jen pulled Terri close for a last hug. As hard as it was, she followed Terri and Bobby to the front door, and closed it once they had pulled away in Bobby's car. "God I hate this part," she offered quietly to Snickers and Jojo as they watched her lean back against the closed door. Somehow, deep down, Jen knew that they shared her concern.

CHAPTER NINETEEN

It always looked so easy when they did it in the movies. Denny continued to shake in her seat in the back of the Lincoln limo. Trying to send a text message from the phone in the pocket of your pants wasn't as simple as Matt Damon made it look in the movies. Especially when the big guy with the gun seemed to want to do nothing but watch her. Oh, and talk about himself. She looked to Faith for, what? Something. Support, understanding, anything, but all she could see was wide-eyed concern—*she's afraid, Robertson*—and something else. Maybe remorse. Denny wasn't sure, but she somehow sensed that everything had gotten away from Faith, and that they were now both in exactly the same boat, a rather leaky boat that was quickly filling with water and captained by a crazy dude with a gun.

She had no idea what it meant when Gun Dude told the driver to head for the warehouse, but since the FBI had been following Faith, Denny took a chance that Agent McKinnon would know what the message meant. She could only hope that she'd actually sent the message to Dr. R's phone and didn't hit the down arrow one too many times and send a cryptic, possibly-misspelled text message to Aunt Betty's home phone. That would suck.

Denny attempted to force down the panic that she was feeling. It didn't help much, especially considering that she was currently experiencing a level of scared that she'd never imagined before. Make it right? She was pretty sure that any making of anything right was pretty much out the window. Hanging on and hoping for the best was about all that Denny had left.

"Ms. Robertson? You don't have much to say."

Oh, shit. He was still talking and now he was talking to her. She looked up, tears brimming in her eyes, to see what the hell he wanted now.

"What do you want from me?" she asked.

"I just need you to show me how you managed to get into my system."

The look on Denny's face must have telegraphed her towering disbelief at what she had just heard. Gun Dude just looked at her, finally coming to the realization that she really hadn't been listening to him before.

"Ah, Ms. Robertson, you're confused. I think I understand. I just wanted to make sure that my network was secure, and you've shown me, in no uncertain terms, that it's not."

"Of course she's confused, you idiot," Faith interjected, showing little concern for the gun that was still pointed in her direction. "You, or whoever the fuck you were pretending to be, hired me to find a kid to break into your system. She really is as naïve as she acts." Faith hesitated, offering her next comment directly toward Denny. "Right, D?"

Denny only nodded.

"She doesn't know squat between terrorism and all that bullshit about Kazakhstan. She doesn't even read the news. You wanted wet-behind-the-ears, and that's exactly what I delivered. She knows all about firewalls and all that techno babble that you love to throw around, but—"

Denny watched with horror as Skip pulled the gun back up level with the side of Faith's head. "Faith, I think you need to shut up now."

Denny's terror grew as Faith reacted to Skip's increased threat. "Knock it off, dude." She reached up, left-handed, to push the barrel of the gun away from her head. "I got you exactly what you asked for, and now you're playing all this *Mission Impossible* bullshit, what with the gun and the limo... Dude. Not cool."

Denny was dumbfounded, and she could guess from the look on Gun Dude's face, that he was right there with her.

"Listen, right now I'm the only thing that the cops have to tie any crime to. I'm the one who smoked the FBI, remember? Which wasn't easy, believe me, especially considering that you were the one who tied them to my tail in the first place. I did everything just the way you asked me to, and now, despite the fact that you lied to me, I get that it's just part of the gig." She stopped talking to point across the back of the car toward Denny. "I got you your hacker, just like you wanted. I lost the FBI, just like you paid me to do, and now you turn on me, too. Bad form, what's your real name...Skip? Dude, you need a new nickname if you're going to do this international terrorism shit."

Denny watched the interplay between Skip and Faith, barely able to comprehend what was transpiring. "Okay, Skip... here's what you need to do. First, put the cannon away. You're scaring the hell out of the kid." Denny could hardly believe her eyes as Skip actually lowered his weapon, resting it, still clutched in his right hand, on the seat of the car. "Good choice. Second, you're going to have Tony pull this overgrown Ford over and let me the fuck out. First rule of international terrorism, Buckwheat: don't fuck over your help. You wanted to see if your system was secure, and we know now that it's not, but I'm just as guilty as you are here, despite the fact the FBI only knows about me and not you. I'm the one part of your plan that's still intact, and keeping me here only makes you look like an amateur. You don't want that now, do you, Skip?"

Denny could plainly see the indecision playing out on Skip's face as he contemplated Faith's words. Words that did nothing but confuse her. Faith was trying to talk her way out of the back of the limo, and it was starting to look to Denny like it was going to work. He wasn't answering quickly enough for Faith, however, who continued to work Skip like the professional criminal that Denny was quickly beginning to realize had duped her just as effectively.

"C'mon, dude. This is stupid. Either shoot me now and show the kid exactly how deep all this shit is, or let me out of this fucking car so I can get back to work."

Denny couldn't believe what was happening. She watched Skip's finger move idly around the trigger guard of his weapon, wondering if he was actually going to blow Faith's brains out. She could see the resolve play across his face as he slid the gun into the pocket of his black jacket.

"Tony, pull over."

Oh, shit.

***

Terri craned her neck to look around the exterior of the warehouse, silently wishing that they had thought to borrow Jen's 4Runner rather than take Bobby's forty-year-old muscle car with the really loud V-8 engine. Since she had no idea if they were actually in the right place, she worried and fumed, looking around for any sign that Denny might be nearby. She could only assume that things had gotten away from Denny, evidenced by the cryptic text message, and she hoped that whoever had shot McNally hadn't shown up to do the same to Denny.

Terri was jarred from her thoughts as Bobby stopped the car, lightly grabbing the sleeve of her jacket with one hand, pointing out the windshield of the car with the other. "Terri, look... limo... over there behind that Dumpster."

She spotted the car even before Bobby got all of the words out. "Yeah, I see it. Circle around the back of the building and check it out. I'm going inside."

Once again, Terri was out of the car and moving, ignoring Bobby's plea for her to wait. Now was hardly the time for a long discussion about procedures. She pulled her weapon from its holster at the small of her back and slid around the side of the building. She had some knowledge of the layout of the building thanks to the surveillance cameras that the Bureau had placed there earlier, but McNally's actions had made access to those cameras impossible. "I'd really like to be able to see what the hell is in there," Terri mused to herself, as she pushed lightly on the first door she reached, hoping that she wasn't walking into a trap.

She took a second to allow her vision to make the adjustment from the bright sunshine outside to the hollow, dark interior of the warehouse, and slipped through the door, hiding in the shadows until she reached a stack of crates large enough to hide behind. She took a moment to catch her breath and try to determine if anyone else was inside the building. The dim illumination spilling in from the skylights of the warehouse did little to make her task easier, but the darkness and shadows provided an oddly comforting sense of security. If she couldn't see them, then they couldn't see her either. She felt her anxiety reduce to a slow simmer. She leaned around the closest crate to look toward the back of the building. The light filtering out from under a door in the back offered hope that someone was here, and if Terri was lucky, it was Denny and she was safe. For the moment anyway. Terri moved stealthily toward the light, quickly realizing that there was no way to safely see who or what was behind the door. She'd have to draw them out.

She looked around through the shadows for something, quickly spotting what she had been looking for. A large metal toolbox sitting on the floor next to a forklift. She dropped into a crouch and moved toward the tools. Hopefully, it would be the distraction that she needed.

***

"What was that?" Skip turned his attention from Denny, who was attempting to explain the holes in his firewall, to the noise that he had heard out in the warehouse. Skip startled as Denny attempted to call out for help, regaining his composure quickly, turning around to level his Glock right at the bridge of her nose. Denny gasped once and firmly closed her mouth, taking his warning seriously.

"Not a sound, Ms. Robertson. Okay?"

Denny nodded quickly, letting Skip know that his message had gotten through. He pulled the door of the office open just enough to slip through and out into the shadows of the warehouse.

***

Terri saw motion as the door opened just wide enough for a tall guy with salt-and-pepper gray hair to step out, gun clutched securely in his right hand. She watched as he turned back, offering a statement that Terri couldn't hear to someone in the office. She could only hope that it was Denny and that she wouldn't freak out when she saw Terri and start yelling. Terri had no idea what to expect as she lobbed another wrench toward the opposite end of the warehouse, watched the sound register to the tall guy with the gun, and silently encouraged him to go check out the noise.

Once he was safely clear of the door and heading toward the diversion that Terri had provided, she stayed low and snuck through the shadows around more stacks of crates, toward the office door. She almost jumped out of her skin when her earpiece crackled to life as Bobby checked in.

"Terri, come in."

"Jesus, Bobby," she hissed into the sleeve of her jacket as she ducked further into the nearest shadow. "Don't do that."

"Sorry. Just wanted to let you know that I arrested the driver of the limo. He said that his boss is inside with Denny."

"Roger that, Bobby. I just got him out of the office and I'm going to check on Denny."

"Got it, Terri. Backup is on the way, so check back in when you know more."

"Okay. Out."

With that, Terri ended the conversation and turned her attention back toward the door to the office after a quick glance over her shoulder to make sure that the tall guy with the gun was still headed the opposite direction. Assured of her safety for the moment, Terri moved quietly toward the door, steeling her nerves to deal with what she could only assume was a terrified Denny who would most likely freak when she spotted the FBI.

If she hadn't been so on edge, Terri would have laughed at the wide-eyed expression of shock on Denny's face as she slid around the corner and into the office. Denny's quivering lower lip and eyes brimming with tears made Terri wonder if Denny was close to an emotional meltdown that would have drawn the attention of everyone within a two-mile radius. That was the last thing either of them needed. Holding a finger to her lips, Terri urged Denny to remain silent as she tried to come up with a way to get her out of the office and outside to safety.

"Are you okay? Did he hurt you?" Terri asked in as low a whisper as she could muster.

"No, I'm all right. He got Faith to call me, and—"

"Tell me all about it later. Right now, we need to get you out of here. He's not going to be gone long."

Denny nodded as Terri pulled her from the chair and urged her down low to the ground, stopping her as Denny tried to reach for her backpack.

"Just leave it. We can get it later," Terri ordered over her shoulder as Denny slid in behind her. She made a quick survey of the area to make sure that the tall guy with the gun was still at the other end of the building. Satisfied that he was occupied long enough to get out of the office, Terri snuck low out the door and over to the shadow at the base of the closest stack of crates, pulling Denny along by the sleeve of her sweatshirt.

Terri was getting more and more nervous as she came to realize that she now had absolutely no idea of the whereabouts of the guy with the gun, but she forced it down long enough to point the way toward the exit and get Denny moving in the right direction.

"Get out that door. The limo is parked around the other side of the building and Agent Kraft is out there. Go find him and tell him what's going on in here." Terri startled as she heard something at the other end of the building. "Go...now!" She gave Denny a rough shove toward the exit and turned to see where the noise had come from.

Terri fought the urge to give in to her fear and follow Denny out the door, but knew that if she did that, it meant that there was no going back. She'd be done, defeated by the demons, proving to everyone that she was incapable of doing the job that she had been so good at for so long. She took a deep breath, swallowed her fear, and allowed her years of training and experience to take over, as she headed back toward the source of the noise.

Scooting quietly from crate to crate, hanging low in the shadows, Terri made her way back toward the office. She assumed that the guy with the gun would return to check on Denny when he found nothing but a couple of misplaced wrenches on the floor. The fact that she was currently unaware of his location did nothing to calm her nerves. The sound of his voice carrying through the semi-darkness broke the last bit of calm that she had.

"I know you're out there."

Terri remained silent, hanging close to the shadow of the nearest stack of crates, fighting against the anxiety that raged through every nerve in her body and threatened to shatter her control.

"I know you're the FBI. I bet you're one of Bulldog's agents. If I'm lucky, you're Agent McKinnon, the head case that he told me all about."

She scuttled around the corner of the crates as she heard the voice getting closer to her comfortable shadow, wondering how he knew about her. Tightening the sweaty grip on her P-228, Terri moved further around the edge of the crates as she tried to determine the big guy's location. If she could see him, she'd have a target, but he was working the shadows just as effectively as she was. Maybe if she could just keep him talking, she could find him before he found her.

"What if I am?" she asked loudly, hoping to goad him into revealing his location.

He laughed. Too long, the smug bastard. "Then I'm in pretty good shape. Your boss told me that you can't be trusted to take the shot."

Damn. That maddeningly smooth voice was starting to piss her off. It was never good when the bad guys knew too much, and this guy definitely fell into that category.

Keep him talking, Terri.

"So, Mr. Whoever-you-are, you know my boss?"

"You can call me Skip. Bulldog and I were old friends."

"Were?"

"Well, things happen sometimes."

"Things?" Terri asked loudly as she moved, crouched low, into the shadow of another stack of crates. "What kind of things?"

"You know, Agent McKinnon. The kind of things that happen when your agents screw up and lose the person that they were supposed to be following."

Damn. This Skip guy really did know too much. Terri realized quickly that she could use that fact to her advantage if she asked the right questions.

"So, these things you're talking about wouldn't happen to involve shooting an old friend in the head, would they?"

More laughter. Cocky bastard. "Please, Agent McKinnon. Don't think that I'm that stupid."

Well, it was worth a try. Terri crouched quietly in the shadows, contemplating her next move. She could call Bobby for help, but more cops would likely only send this guy over the edge. Since a shootout in a dark warehouse sounded like a really bad idea, she opted instead to simply keep moving and hope that he revealed himself before he found her. Besides, she could handle this. It was her job, what she was trained to do.

Terri stood up, hanging close to the crate, staying hidden in the shadows. She started to call out with another question to see if she could flush him out, but got way more than she had anticipated. As she craned her neck around the side of the crate, she noticed movement right in front of her face. She tried to duck, but it was already too late as her brain managed to process a hand clutching a gun in that second right before it made contact with her face. Stunned, she fell backward, landing hard on her back, immediately becoming aware of the metallic tang of blood in her mouth.

Not good, Terri.

Fighting against the stars swimming across her field of vision, Terri tried to take inventory. Her teeth seemed to be intact, but her lip was split open and bleeding freely. She thought about trying to sit up, but Skip's gun pointed at her face pretty much made the decision for her. Skip towered over her as she lay on the ground.

"So, Agent McKinnon, here we are."

Terri remained silent, hoping that whatever this guy was going to do, that he'd do it quickly. Her hand tightened and relaxed around the grip of her own weapon, but there was no way she could raise it quickly enough to get the drop on him.

"Are you going to shoot me, Agent McKinnon? That's what you're supposed to do, right? Shoot the bad guy."

Terri froze. Could she do that? Could she really pull the trigger and end one more life?

"C'mon, Agent McKinnon." He lowered the gun and spread his arms wide, offering her a clear target. "Bulldog told me that you were a head case and it sure looks to me like he was right."

Terri lifted her gun from the floor. As hard as she tried, she couldn't stop her hand from shaking. Voices played through her head as tried to pull it together.

I can't put you out there with a loaded weapon in your hands... Why didn't you call for backup? I can't be sure that you'll use it if the situation requires it... I've had to listen to all the locker room bullshit about Defective Agent McKinnon... I'm beginning to think that they were right about you.

Images joined the voices. Memories of breaking glass and blood. Nightmare images of Jen, bloodied and dead. A phantom ache in her side where the bullet had struck and broken her ribs. The taste of blood in her mouth.

After what seemed like hours spent in the horror of her own thoughts, Terri gave up and let her gun hand fall back to the floor. The overwhelming realization that she was now basically screwed and at his mercy only got worse as Skip tossed his head back and howled. If he laughed any harder he was going to split something, she thought miserably.

"I guess Bulldog was right about you, Agent McKinnon" He leveled the gun and Terri could see every detail of the square end of the small Austrian automatic pistol. "There's really nothing you can do to stop me now, is there?"

"Guess again, asshole!"

Terri registered the sound of the unfamiliar voice just before she saw the movement behind Skip. Before he could react, Terri saw what appeared to be something in the neighborhood of about four feet of galvanized steel pipe come slicing through the air at tremendous speed, stopping with a sickening crunch when it made contact with the side of Skip's skull. There wasn't even time for Skip to register the impact before he was falling to the side, making absolutely no attempt to break his own fall. Terri watched him land almost on top of her before turning her attention to the spot above her where his face used to be. She recognized the dark hair, deep brown eyes, and black leather jacket of her savior.

Faith.

Terri knew that the gape-mouthed expression on her own face completely telegraphed her surprise at what had just transpired. Faith relieved Terri of the responsibility of having to speak with her next words.

"Are you okay?"

Terri nodded as she sat up, still dumbstruck as Faith tossed the length of pipe aside, crossed her arms over her ample breasts, and waited for an answer.

"Yeah, I'm fine. What the...?"

"Assholes like him"—Faith motioned toward Skip's unconscious form on the floor—"give all of us a bad name. I warned him not to fuck with me."

"But you...him... what about Denny?"

"Ah, D's a good kid. She fucked up, no thanks to me, but ol' Skip here told her the whole story. She'll fill you in."

"But what about you? You hired her. Are you turning yourself in?"

Faith wrapped an arm around her belly and laughed. It was a joyous sound that almost made Terri join in, despite the surreal nature of the whole conversation.

"Um, no. I figure you owe me one for taking care of that..." Faith pointed toward Skip who was still not moving. "So I think maybe I should just walk right out of here, and we'll call it even. How's that work for you?"

Looking over at Skip's motionless form, Terri dismissed it quickly to turn her full attention back toward Faith. She thought for a moment while she checked her lip, noting the smear of blood across the back of her hand. "Go, now. Hurry, before I change my mind." Terri couldn't believe the words had come out of her mouth, but they had, and there was no going back now.

Faith grinned and offered one last comment. "Just for future reference, the next time you go undercover, wear your sneakers. The black shoes give the cop thing away every time."

With that, Faith waved good-bye and headed toward the back door of the warehouse.

Despite her split lip, Terri quirked a smile and spoke into the sleeve of her jacket. "Bobby, suspect is down. Are the EMTs here yet?"

She could hear the near-palpable relief in his voice. "Yeah, Terri. They arrived a few minutes ago. We're coming in."

"Roger that, Bobby," Terri answered as she pulled herself up off the floor by hanging onto a nearby crate. The sound of a door closing in the back was soon overwhelmed by the sounds of the EMTs, Bobby, and the rest of the force that he'd managed to muster in support. Terri turned her attention toward the back door one last time, wondering if she'd ever see Faith again. As she gingerly probed at the cut on her lip with her fingers, Terri came to the full realization that just about anything was possible.

Chapter Twenty

Terri...he's here!"

Stopping one last time to check her appearance in the bathroom mirror, Terri registered Jen's announcement of Bobby's arrival to pick her up. She frowned, noting the bruises around her mouth, stitches in her lower lip, and decided that pistol-whipped was not a great look for her. Nothing she could do about it now. She adjusted her weapon in the holster at the small of her back, pulled her jacket down and fiddled with the collar of her freshly ironed white shirt, making sure that everything was just right before heading down the steps.

"Terri..."

"I'm coming," she called out as she pounded down the steps. "Did you fix me some—"

"Coffee," Jen answered as she held out a stainless steel travel mug. "Just like you like it."

Terri smiled as best she could, feeling the pull of the stitches in her lip as she accepted her coffee. "Thanks, sweetie. I'll be home early, so if you want to do something after work—"

"Baby, I can still go with you. It's just a faculty meeting, and I can play hooky if you need me to."

Terri gave up trying to smile. It wasn't working anyway. "Jen, it's just something I have to do for work. Go to your meeting. I'll be fine."

"Okay," Jen offered tentatively.

"Really, Jen," Terri said, pleading her case, as she set her travel mug down on the table next to the front door. "I'll be okay. I'll have a chance to talk to Bobby, I'll get this thing done, and I promise we'll talk about it later."

Terri walked slowly down the steps outside, slipping on her sunglasses as a defense against the late October sunshine. The day was mild, maybe a little chilly, the kind of day that Terri loved. Spending the day outside with a good book, wrapped in a bulky sweater as the leaves swirled and danced in the park would have been nice, but work came first today. She offered Bobby a quiet "good morning" as she pulled the car door open, sliding into the passenger seat of his Firebird as he gunned the engine and pulled away from the curb. Bobby returned her greeting quietly as she buckled her seat belt and settled in to start working on her coffee. She sputtered a little as the hot liquid hit the stitches in her lip.

"So, Terri, how's the lip this morning?"

"Actually, Bobby, it feels like someone popped me in the mouth with the butt end of a Glock."

Bobby laughed and continued to drive. "Speaking of the Glock, I got a call from Ballistics and they positively identified the Glock that busted you in the chops as McNally's murder weapon. I guess that takes care of that. Not like there's much we can do about it."

"Why? Is there news about that Skip guy? Is he still out

of it?"

"Yeah, and it looks like he's going to stay that way for a while. Faith tagged him a good one. We still have a guard on the door in the ICU, but he's not going anywhere, possibly ever again. Pretty significant brain damage."

"Yeah," Terri said, not wanting to get too far into any conversations about Faith. She still had some reservations about letting her go, but Terri knew full well that Faith had saved her life, and that usually served to make things complicated. "What about Denny? Any news from the Federal prosecutor?"

"Well, Terri, that's an interesting situation. Since the guy she committed the crime against is the person who hired her to commit the crime, there's really nothing to prosecute. Looks like she got lucky. It helps that she gave us the heads-up. Too bad Faith is missing."

"Um-hum," Terri answered quietly as she looked out the window of the car toward the office buildings lining both sides of Connecticut Avenue. "I figure she's gone for good. I'm still not sure about letting her go like I did, but..."

"I probably would have done the same thing. The official report only says that she got away and that seems to have satisfied everyone at the office, so don't worry about it anymore, okay?"

"Okay," Terri answered, relieved by Bobby's reassurance of her actions. "Anyway, Jen asked about Denny this morning. She still hasn't heard from her and she's concerned."

Bobby changed lanes to get onto the bridge leading to Northern Virginia. "She's not pissed?"

"Well, she was for a while, but we had a pretty long talk about it. It's not Denny's fault that I got hurt, but I don't blame Jen for being a little pissed. She did, after all, try to tell Denny that hacking for cash was a bad idea. Oh, and the way she took off without telling anybody... I mean, everything turned out okay, but still..."

"It made a pretty huge mess for everyone, but it is a good thing that Denny found the stuff about the bioterrorism."

"Well, that is good." Terri wondered how many more people like Skip were out there, cooking up stuff to hurt large numbers of people. Bobby stayed silent as he drove, leaving Terri alone with her thoughts until they reached their destination. There was a lot more that she needed to say, but there were things to do first.

***

Terri stood quietly in the bright sunshine, comforted by the close proximity of Bobby to her right and Dave Stansfield to her left. Despite her sunglasses, she lowered her head against the brightness of the light. The line of FBI agents that extended to either side of her, all decked in their best black suits, provided an odd sense of comfort. Looking around as much as she could without appearing like an undisciplined cadet, Terri noted that she wasn't the only one this morning who had taken the extra time to polish their shoes. Sometimes, respect required that you looked your best. Despite the nasty cut and bruises that made her look like she'd taken a pistol butt to the mouth, which seemed appropriate considering that she had, Terri knew that she presented the picture of a professional law enforcement agent.

Too bad she didn't feel like one anymore.

The sound of a voice behind her pulled Terri from her

musings. "Ready...fire."

Terri steeled herself not to jump too much at the sound as seven rifles discharged in unison. The voice repeated the orders two more times, the rifles responding each time, until they were commanded to "order arms." She was okay, really, until the sound of a lone bugler, hidden somewhere over a rise, began to play "Taps." That's when she really felt like she might lose it, so she balled up her fists and willed herself not to cry. The voice of the minister in front of her provided the distraction she needed to get herself back under control.

"...as we commend the body of our friend, George Edward McNally, to the ground...ashes to ashes, dust to dust."

Terri could only focus on the sound of the minister's voice, not the actual words, as she looked up toward the casket poised over a cement-lined hole in the ground. It really was that simple, wasn't it? One day you're here, and the next day you're not. Well, it seemed that simple until Terri caught sight of Helen McNally, seated front row center, tears streaming down her face as she accepted the American flag, neatly folded into a perfect triangle by the Marine Corps Honor Guard. The picture was that of the perfect American family, as a tall, broad-shouldered young man placed a loving hand on the back of his mother's neck and a younger girl, somewhere around fourteen or fifteen years old, took her mother's hand. Terri wasn't sure if their actions were to provide or to receive comfort, but it didn't really matter, did it? A woman had lost her husband, and two children had lost their father with one squeeze of the trigger in the hand of a nutjob with delusions of ruling the world. It was all just so...

"...senseless. That's what it is, Terri. It's senseless. She was *only forty-seven years old. It just don't seem right, losing her this way." Terri wasn't even sure who was saying that to her. Again. How many times would she have to listen to people tell her that it was senseless?*

"Your momma was always so lovely to everyone."

"Your momma always had a fresh cup of coffee for me."

"Your momma loved you so much, Terri."

Terri fought the urge to run away, far away, screaming her way into the small patch of woods on the south end of the farm. It was her place, her special quiet spot, where she could read a big, thick book about some far-off, wonderful place, populated by characters that always knew the difference between right and wrong. She'd sit for hours, wrapped in her favorite bulky sweater as the leaves swirled and danced around the base of the tree that supported her back and shoulders, barely noticing the damp ground beneath her that usually left a large patch of wet denim stuck securely to her butt. She would lose herself in the book, cheering to herself when the bad guy would screw up and get caught by the good guy. The good guy beat the bad guy, every time, because right is always right and wrong loses every time.

That's how it works, right?

As much as she loved her detective stories, Terri would often slam the book shut in disgust, especially at the end, the part where the doe-eyed ingénue professed her undying love and gratitude to the brave, strong, handsome, and always male detective who had just saved her life. Terri didn't want to be the ingénue; she wanted to be the detective, had wanted that for as long as she could remember. She hoped that someday the ingénue would look at her that way, puppy-dog eyes brimming with grateful tears, telling her that she was strong and brave and wonderful and all those other positive things that represented the good guy in the story.

Someday.

But not today. Today, Terri had to bury her mother. On a glorious fall day, somewhere in the flatlands of central Ohio, a sixteen-year-old girl had to sit outside, next to an open grave in a cold metal folding chair that was covered with some really ugly funeral home fabric. She had to be strong for her daddy, take care of her brother, and bury her mother.

It just didn't seem fair.

All of the pink ribbons in the world couldn't cushion the blow of the breast cancer that had ravaged her mother's body. She too, had taken her father's hand, while her older brother had stood behind, silently, like a statue. Terri had heard her daddy, crying, actually sobbing in the bathroom sometime during the night, but that was gone now.

"You have to be strong, Terri."

"People don't need to know your trouble, Terri."

"Be good to your daddy when I'm gone, Terri. He loves you so much."

She had heard her brother, Donnie, stumble in a little while later, slamming the back door to the mudroom, staggering under the effects of what Terri knew to be copious amounts of Jim Beam and Budweiser. She listened downstairs, cringing at the sound, as all of the bourbon and beer made an ugly return visit, forcing Donnie to vomit into the kitchen sink, too drunk and sick to make it upstairs to the bathroom.

"You have to be strong, Terri."

"People don't need to know your trouble, Terri."

"Take care of Donnie when I'm gone, Terri. He's not strong like you."

She had no idea, on that bright fall day, of how her mother's death would change her and the two men in her family, but it had in many huge ways. Her father had never been the same since that day. Neither had her brother, and she supposed that she hadn't either, but things do indeed change, and often not for the better.

Lost in her own memories, Terri hadn't realized that the funeral was over until she felt a comforting hand at the back of her neck. She didn't even need to turn around to know that Bobby was behind her.

"Terri, are you okay?"

"Yeah," she said, "I'm fine." She'd said the words, actually believed them in some part of her brain, but she still couldn't tear her eyes away from Helen McNally, as the brave widow accepted handshakes and hugs from what Terri could only assume were extended family members.

It's all so senseless.

She leaned into the comfort that Bobby was offering, finally tearing her gaze away from the McNally family to turn and accept a hug from the person who had been her best friend for most of her adult life. In the solid, safe embrace of Bobby's arms, she finally let go of the tears that she'd been holding on to. He stood silently, rubbing small circles on her back until the flood of emotion seemed to run itself out and Terri could finally speak.

"It's just so stupid."

"Yeah, Terri, it's just about the most stupid thing I can imagine. But it could have been a whole lot worse, you know?

I can't help but think how close we came to losing you this time. You've got to stop with the close call thing. I can't take it anymore."

"I know, Bobby, and that's why I'm taking an extended leave." She looked up and noted the expression on Bobby's face. Relief, perhaps, but not an ounce of surprise.

"I think that's a great idea. What are you going to do?"

"I'm not really sure, Bobby. I'm going to take a long nap when I get home, and then I'm going to call the therapist at the Bureau and see if I can really fix things this time. No more saying the right things just to try to shortcut my way out of trouble. I'm serious this time. I'm going to fix things for myself or maybe I'll find out that this is something that I can't fix, and move on. I just don't know right now."

"Well, sweetie, you know my number, and you know that I'll always be there for anything you need. Hell, maybe you'll be back to full form in a couple of months and we can get back to business as usual. That would be great."

Terri looked out across the perfectly aligned rows of grave markers at the cemetery, trying to focus her gaze anywhere other than back toward Helen McNally. She took one long breath, blew it out, and answered, "Yeah, Bobby, it sure would. But I tend to think that business as usual isn't what it used to be."

"No, it definitely isn't, but I wouldn't change a thing."

Terri could hardly believe her ears. "You wouldn't?"

"No, Terri, I wouldn't. You've found someone incredibly special and I can only hope to meet someone someday who looks at me the way she looks at you. You're amazingly lucky that you found her, and no job in the world is worth losing that kind of happiness. And you know, if I lose you as a partner because of it, well then so be it. I know, deep down, that I'll never lose you as a friend, and that's the most important thing."

Terri snuggled back into Bobby's arms, failing at another attempt to keep the tears at bay. "You really are too good to be true, Agent Kraft."

"Well, maybe, but you're right up there too, Agent McKinnon." Bobby offered one last squeeze, releasing the embrace to take Terri by the shoulders. "So before things get way too mushy for me, I need to get back to the office. Besides, there's someone else here that I think you need to go talk to." Bobby gently urged Terri to turn around. She immediately spotted Jen, standing off to the side, car keys in one hand, looking a little uncomfortable as she shifted her weight from foot to foot. Terri reached behind, offering Bobby one last squeeze of her hand before he turned to leave.

Terri crossed the space between the rows of markers quickly to get to Jen and wrapped her arms around her. With that simple embrace, Terri came to the full realization that Bobby had been right about all of it. She was the luckiest person on the planet and it was all thanks to Jen. She had a million things that she wanted to say, but none of them wanted to fully form themselves into words, so Terri let it all go to enjoy the feeling of Jen's arms around her. Jen broke the comfortable silence with a question.

"I know you really wanted me to go to my meeting today, but I just couldn't. Is everything all right with you?"

Terri smiled into Jen's neck, not wanting to let go. "Yeah, sweetie, I think it is. Especially now that you're here. That was a nice surprise."

"Yeah, well, I hoped it would be. You can be a little stubborn, you know, so I called Bobby while you were in the shower this morning and worked it out. He thought it was a good idea too. That way, you could get all the low down from him on the way out here, and I could take you home."

"Why is it, for someone who thinks that she's such a spaz, that you always know the right thing to say or do?"

"Well, I don't really know." Jen waved off the question. "Just some kind of emotional idiot savant thing that I do, I suppose. So, how did Bobby take the news?"

"He thought it was a good idea." Terri took Jen by the hand to lead her out of the cemetery and back to the car. "He hopes that I can fix everything up and get back to work, but I think he'll be okay if I don't."

"Of course he'll be okay, baby. He only wants you to be happy."

"Yeah, Jen, I know that. I only want that for him too."

"Baby, you know something? You don't always have to be strong for everyone else." Jen looked up, puppy-dog eyes brimming with loving tears. "You're strong and brave and wonderful, but now's the time to take care of Terri. She really deserves that, you know?"

"Yeah, but that's hard for me. I guess I need to put that on the list of things to work on." Jen placed a protective arm around Terri's shoulders, urging her again to start walking toward the car. A small thought began to form in the back of Terri's mind, offering her a bit of insight to her own problems. "You know, Jen, I think I figured out something this morning."

"What's that, baby?"

"First, I really hate funerals, but I learned something. This job, this thing that I do..." Terri hesitated, finally finding the words to explain exactly what she was feeling, "... this thing that I am requires that I leave the house every day, never knowing if today's the day that I don't get to come home." She felt Jen shudder under her hand. "I was okay with that. Part of the gig, you know? But that's all changed now. I stood there this morning, with all that stuff..." Terri hesitated, waving her hand in the air to emphasize her point. "...the expensive casket, the bugler, the twenty-one-gun salute, everyone from the office, all of it. With all of that going on, I still couldn't take my eyes off Helen McNally."

"What do you mean, baby?"

"I mean that I think my problem is fairly simple. As long as I was alone, death seemed easy. Bobby would miss me, but he'd go on. My dad hasn't said more than six sentences to me, hell, to anyone since Mom died, and Donnie... well, Donnie's a mess and I don't think that all of the AA meetings and Serenity Prayers in the world are going to help him. But now..."

"But now what?"

"But now, I have you to think about. I can handle the idea of me winding up in the box, but I can't... no, I won't put you in that chair. I've been there, and it just hurts too damn much. Jen, you deserve so much more than to be the brave Widow Rosenberg. You deserve to be happy and loved and I want to be there for you for as long as possible."

Jen stopped walking when they reached her 4Runner. Terri turned to lean against the fender of the car, felt Jen's small hands grab the front of her black jacket and pull her close. "You know something else, Agent McKinnon? You're an amazing person, and just about the time I decide that I couldn't possibly love you any more, you say or do something that shows me that I'm wrong."

"Did I just do that?"

"Yeah, you big doofus, you did. Baby, I fell in love with a cop, and I understand what that means. I try not to think about it too much, because there's nothing I can do about it, but I've always understood that what you do for a living is dangerous. I was willing to take that leap because I love you. If I do wind up in that chair someday, well, then I do, but I'll be okay because I got to love you and make you happy too. It's not like I'd get all psycho-crazy and try to blow up the world or something equally stupid."

"Well, yeah, that would be kind of stupid."

"Yes, it would, but right now I'm scared that you'll go out there and get yourself killed because you're worrying about me, and I can't have that any more than you can handle the idea of putting me in that chair. So we'll fix this and we'll do it together. Sound like a plan?"

"Sweetie, that sounds like a great idea. Then maybe I can go be a cop again and—"

"Terri, you know I love you, but you need to understand that I'll still love you even if you find out that you can't be a cop anymore. I didn't fall in love with a cop. I fell in love with you."

Terri fell in love all over again. Words left her as she reached up, taking Jen's hands in her own and leaned in, offering her a tentative, gentle kiss. Jen's soft voice in her ear told Terri that everything would indeed be okay. "But you'll still wear the cargo pants for me, won't you?"

Terri threw her head back and laughed. "You know something, Jen. You never disappoint me." Terri released Jen and backed away to climb into the passenger seat of the green 4Runner. Watching out the windshield as Jen crossed in front of the car to hop into the driver's seat, Terri realized that she was indeed the luckiest woman on the planet. After Jen buckled her seat belt, Terri slipped her sunglasses back on and watched as a small hand reached across the space between the seats, touching Terri lightly on the thigh. Jen turned to her and asked, "So now what do we do, Agent McKinnon?"

The answer was so simple and so right.

"Take me home, Dr. Rosenberg."

About the Author

D.L. Line has been many things at different times in her life: a musician, a pharmacy technician, a bartender, a student, a restaurant owner, a marching band director, and a dog sitter to name a few. Through it all, she has always been a storyteller.

D.L. lives in Ohio with her family, including Snickers the Wonderdog.

Books Available from Bold Strokes Books

One Last Thing by Kim Baldwin & Xenia Alexiou. Blood is thicker than pride. The final book in the Elite Operative Series brings together foes, family, and friends to start a new order. (978-1-62639-230-4)

Songs Unfinished by Holly Stratimore. Two aspiring rock stars learn that falling in love while pursuing their dreams can be harmonious—if they can only keep their pasts from throwing them out of tune. (978-1-62639-231-1)

Beyond the Ridge by L.T. Marie. Will a contractor and a horse rancher overcome their family differences and find common ground to build a life together? (978-1-62639-232-8)

Swordfish by Andrea Bramhall. Four women battle the demons from their pasts. Will they learn to let go, or will happiness be forever beyond their grasp? (978-1-62639-233-5)

The Fiend Queen by Barbara Ann Wright. Princess Katya and her consort Starbride must turn evil against evil in order to banish Fiendish power from their kingdom, and only love will pull them back from the brink. (978-1-62639-234-2)

Up the Ante by PJ Trebelhorn. When Jordan Stryker and Ashley Noble meet again fifteen years after a short-lived affair, are either of them prepared to gamble on a chance at love? (978-1-62639-237-3)

Speakeasy by MJ Williamz. When mob leader Helen Byrne sets her sights on the girlfriend of Al Capone's right-hand man, passion and tempers flare on the streets of Chicago. (978-1-62639-238-0)

Venus in Love by Tina Michele. Morgan Blake can't afford any distractions and Ainsley Dencourt can't afford to lose control—but the beauty of life and art usually lies in the unpredictable strokes of the artist's brush. (978-1-62639-220-5)

Rules of Revenge by AJ Quinn. When a lethal operative on a collision course with her past agrees to help a CIA analyst on a critical assignment, the encounter proves explosive in ways neither woman anticipated. (978-1-62639-221-2)

The Romance Vote by Ali Vali. Chili Alexander is a sought-after campaign consultant who isn't prepared when her boss's daughter, Samantha Pellegrin, comes to work at the firm and shakes up Chili's life from the first day. (978-1-62639-222-9)

Advance: Exodus Book One by Gun Brooke. Admiral Dael Caydoc's mission to find a new homeworld for the Oconodian people is hazardous, but working with the infuriating Commander Aniwyn "Spinner" Seclan endangers her heart and soul. (978-1-62639-224-3)

UnCatholic Conduct by Stevie Mikayne. Jil Kidd goes undercover to investigate fraud at St. Marguerite's Catholic School, but life gets complicated when her student is killed—and she begins to fall for her prime target. (978-1-62639-304-2)

Season's Meetings by Amy Dunne. Catherine Birch reluctantly ventures on the festive road trip from hell with beautiful stranger Holly Daniels only to discover the road to true love has its own obstacles to maneuver. (978-1-62639-227-4)

Myth and Magic: Queer Fairy Tales edited by Radclyffe and Stacia Seaman. Myth, magic, and monsters—the stuff of childhood dreams (or nightmares) and adult fantasies. (978-1-62639-225-0)

Nine Nights on the Windy Tree by Martha Miller. Recovering drug addict, Bertha Brannon, is an attorney who is trying to stay clean when a murder sends her back to the bad end of town. (978-1-62639-179-6)

Driving Lessons by Annameekee Hesik. Dive into Abbey Brooks's sophomore year as she attempts to figure out the amazing, but sometimes complicated, life of a you-know-who girl at Gila High School. (978-1-62639-228-1)

Asher's Shot by Elizabeth Wheeler. Asher Price's candid photographs capture the truth, but when his success requires exposing an enemy, Asher discovers his only shot at happiness involves revealing secrets of his own. (978-1-62639-229-8)

Courtship by Carsen Taite. Love and justice—a lethal mix or a perfect match? (978-1-62639-210-6)

Against Doctor's Orders by Radclyffe. Corporate financier Presley Worth wants to shut down Argyle Community Hospital, but Dr. Harper Rivers will fight her every step of the way, if she can also fight their growing attraction. (978-1-62639-211-3)

A Spark of Heavenly Fire by Kathleen Knowles. Kerry and Beth are building their life together, but unexpected circumstances could destroy their happiness. (978-1-62639-212-0)

Never Too Late by Julie Blair. When Dr. Jamie Hammond is forced to hire a new office manager, she's shocked to come face to face with Carla Grant and memories from her past. (978-1-62639-213-7)

Widow by Martha Miller. Judge Bertha Brannon must solve the murder of her lover, a policewoman she thought she'd grow old with. As more bodies pile up, the murderer starts coming for her. (978-1-62639-214-4)

Twisted Echoes by Sheri Lewis Wohl. What's a woman to do when she realizes the voices in her head are real? (978-1-62639-215-1)

Criminal Gold by Ann Aptaker. Through a dangerous night in New York in 1949, Cantor Gold, dapper dyke-about-town, smuggler of fine art, is forced by a crime lord to be his instrument of vengeance. (978-1-62639-216-8)

The Melody of Light by M.L. Rice. After surviving abuse and loss, will Riley Gordon be able to navigate her first year of college and accept true love and family? (978-1-62639-219-9)

Because of You by Julie Cannon. What would you do for the woman you were forced to leave behind? (978-1-62639-199-4)

The Job by Jove Belle. Sera always dreamed that she would one day reunite with Tor. She just didn't think it would involve terrorists, firearms, and hostages. (978-1-62639-200-7)

Making Time by C.J. Harte. Two women going in different directions meet after fifteen years and struggle to reconnect in spite of the past that separated them. (978-1-62639-201-4)

Once The Clouds Have Gone by KE Payne. Overwhelmed by the dark clouds of her past, Tag Grainger is lost until the intriguing and spirited Freddie Metcalfe unexpectedly forces her to reevaluate her life. (978-1-62639-202-1)

The Acquittal by Anne Laughlin. Chicago private investigator Josie Harper searches for the real killer of a woman whose lover has been acquitted of the crime. (978-1-62639-203-8)

An American Queer: The Amazon Trail by Lee Lynch. Lee Lynch's heartening and heart-rending history of gay life from the turbulence of the late 1900s to the triumphs of the early 2000s are recorded in this selection of her columns. (978-1-62639-204-5)

Stick McLaughlin: The Prohibition Years by CF Frizzell. Corruption in 1918 cost Stick her lover, her freedom, and her identity, but a very special flapper and the family bond of her own gang could help win them back—even if it means outwitting the Boston Mob. (978-1-62639-205-2)

Edge of Awareness by C.A. Popovich. When Maria, a woman in the middle of her third divorce, meets Dana, an out lesbian, awareness of her feelings brings up reservations about the teachings of her church. (978-1-62639-188-8)

Taken by Storm by Kim Baldwin. Lives depend on two women when a train derails high in the remote Alps, but an unforgiving mountain, avalanches, crevasses, and other perils stand between them and safety. (978-1-62639-189-5)

The Common Thread by Jaime Maddox. Dr. Nicole Coussart's life is falling apart, but fortunately, DEA Attorney Rae Rhodes is there to pick up the pieces and help Nic put them back together. (978-1-62639-190-1)

Jolt by Kris Bryant. Mystery writer Bethany Lange wasn't prepared for the twisting emotions that left her breathless the moment she laid eyes on folk singer sensation Ali Hart. (978-1-62639-191-8)

Searching For Forever by Emily Smith. Dr. Natalie Jenner's life has always been about saving others, until young paramedic Charlie Thompson comes along and shows her maybe she's the one who needs saving. (978-1-62639-186-4)

A Queer Sort of Justice: Prison Tales Across Time by Rebecca S. Buck. When liberty is only a memory, and all seems lost, what freedoms and hopes can be found within us? (978-1-62639-195-6E)

Blue Water Dreams by Dena Hankins. Lania Marchiol keeps her wary sailor's gaze trained on the horizon until Oly Rassmussen, a wickedly handsome trans man, sends her trusty compass spinning off course. (978-1-62639-192-5)

Rest Home Runaways by Clifford Henderson. Baby boomer Morgan Ronzio's troubled marriage is the least of her worries when she gets the call that her addled, eighty-six-year-old, half-blind dad has escaped the rest home. (978-1-62639-169-7)

Charm City by Mason Dixon. Raq Overstreet's loyalty to her drug kingpin boss is put to the test when she begins to fall for Bathsheba Morris, the undercover cop assigned to bring him down. (978-1-62639-198-7)

Let the Lover Be by Sheree Greer. Kiana Lewis, a functional alcoholic on the verge of destruction, finally faces the demons of her past while finding love and earning redemption in New Orleans. (978-1-62639-077-5)

Blindsided by Karis Walsh. Blindsided by love, guide dog trainer Lenae McIntyre and media personality Cara Bradley learn to trust what they see with their hearts. (978-1-62639-078-2)

About Face by VK Powell. Forensic artist Macy Sheridan and Detective Leigh Monroe work on a case that has troubled them both for years, but they're hampered by the past and their unlikely yet undeniable attraction. (978-1-62639-079-9)

Blackstone by Shea Godfrey. For Darry and Jessa, their chance at a life of freedom is stolen by the arrival of war and an ancient prophecy that just might destroy their love. (978-1-62639-080-5)

Out of This World by Maggie Morton. Iris decided to cross an ocean to get over her ex. But instead, she ends up traveling much farther, all the way to another world. Once there, only a mysterious, sexy, and magical woman can help her return home. (978-1-62639-083-6)

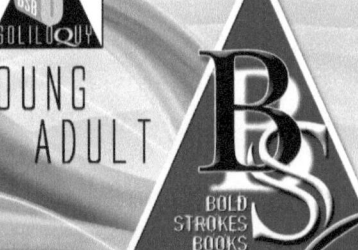